Ou Sanctuary

Sequel to
Amidst the Stones of Fire
by William Siems

Out of the Sanctuary

Copyright © 2018 by William Siems

First printing - July 2018

ISBN: 978-0-9997026-3-5

eISBN: 978-0-9997026-5-9

AudioISBN: 978-0-9997026-6-6

Scripture quotations from the SUV (Siems Unauthorized Version) of the Bible

Contact the author at siemsrj@live.com

Cover by Jacob Bridgman

Interior design by Alane Pearce of ProfessionalWriting Services, LLC MyPublishingCoach.com

Dedication

I never planned on writing two novels, but the ending of "Amidst the Stones of Fire" required a sequel. Besides, since the first novel took 45 years to complete, a second would guarantee that I lived to be almost 105 years old. Well, I finished the the rough draft of the sequel in less than 45 days. I am grateful for all those who helped bring it to the printed page. Of special note, again, are Keith Timmer, my wife Nancy (to whom I read each chapter as I wrote it and who often exclaimed, "You can't leave me there! That's terrible! Tell me what happens next?"), my daughter Angela, and the Liberator (Jesus) whom we all follow.

Table of Contents

(continued on next page)

Preface

The writing of novels is a funny thing. You think you should wait for inspiration, but a wise man told me, forty-some years after I started my first novel, "If you do the hard work, writing every day, inspiration will come." Unfortunately, inspiration is a rather fickle mistress and sometimes you find yourself in the middle of chapter eight and have to figure out how to get your characters from back in chapter four up to that place in the story. That's the work part.

Please remember, this novel is an apocalyptic fantasy, a work of fiction. Any relationship of its characters to real people or events is simply coincidental. Some will not like this novel, as they didn't like its predecessor, and will try to attack its theology. I would simply remind them, "This is not meant to be a theological treatise; it is only a novel." Others might ask, "You don't really believe every thing that you write here, do you?" to which I respond, "My responsibility is to tell this story the best I can, and I hope I have done that part well. What you believe does not need to correspond to what I believe or vice versa, but, hopefully, it matches the truth revealed by the Liberator (Jesus)."

William Siems

July 2018

Note: Hopefully the "Prologue" will provide you the necessary background if you haven't read the first novel or if it's been a long time since you have read it. I have included at the outset a glossary of names of those from the first novel (identified with an *) as well as those who show up in this one. Again, each chapter begins with an epigraph simply because I like them.

Glossary of Names
(*in "Amidst the Stones of Fire")

*Aaron Elias - the prophet, Urim stone of *Lights*

Abdul - former Muslim, 2nd Witness

*Adam - the cat-dog clone (Cog), *Discernment* stone

*Adonis Ashereem - Triparteum's chancellor

*Adrian Quick - Director of the Science Board

*Alathos - the centaur, the Sanctuary's Guardian

Ametz - the name of the stone of Courage

*Anna - a young girl, *Way* stone

*Ark of the Covenant - an ancient Old Testament artifact

*Ayah and Anan - angelic protectors and carriers of the Ark

Azinath - the great eagle

*Baalel - Adonis' personal prophet and medium

*Ben Ha-Chiya-Ra - humanoid son of Adonis, false angel

Beth - Juan Carlos' daughter

*Bigtha - apprentice gardener, Sword Meshar

*Caleb - the dog-next-door in the Sanctuary

Cat - an elite female Triparteum sharpshooter

Cephas - a Sanctuary peacemaker

*Chayeem - the Tree in the middle of Eden's garden

*Christine Andrews - hospital nurse

*Dal (Defiance) - the hawk, *Night* stone

Diggory - Sanctuary gopher

*Eagle (Azinath) - bringer of the *Sanctuary* stone

Eleazar - one of the six captains: Feeding the Hungry

*Gideon Anakim (Dr.)- Scientist, discovered Gideonite

*Gomed Akkub - soldier, renamed Meshar, *Peace* stone/sword

Grandfather - Old Man and teacher of Hash the 1st Witness

*Hail'yk - Archangel R'gel's lost sword

*Hal - (Archangel)Choirmaster of heaven, the Luminescent One

*Hashadiel (Hash) - Julius' & Judy's son, 1st Witness, *Courage*

*Hashamayeem & Meshar - swords made from Hail'yk

Hasees - Worship-gifted swallow

Headquarters (HQ) - Grandfather, Dal, and Hash's Cavern

J1 and J2 - elite Triparteum soldiers

Jacob Laban - Kouta's Lieutenant, farm infiltrator

Joe - Juan Carlos' son, farm worker

Jordan - former Infantry Colonel

*Jon - Bahn's pupil, the Farm's Pastor, *Life* stone

*José - The Saint, itinerant preacher, priest, *Thummin (Truths)* stone

Josephsons - another farm owning family

*Juan Carlos & Maria - farm workers and now owners

*Judy - Jackknife's sister, druggie, becomes José's wife

*Julius - humorist, magician, clown, marries Judy, *Hope* stone

Justice - man with the healing gift

*Kate - the pelican, first finder of the Thummin (*Truths*)

*Kouta - Ben's general

Liberator - Jesus

*Logan - the dwarf, animal whisperer, *Awe* stone

Manasseh - angel, peacemaker

*Mary - Jon's wife, died and revived by Gideonite

Meezimore - one of the six captains (angel), worship gift

*Meshar - Gomed's new name, given the stone/sword of *Peace*

Mishal - one of the six captains (angel), prayer gifted

Mocherah - Blue Team angel

Nathaniel (Nate) - former blind beggar

Ometz - Hash's guardian angel, bringer of the *Courage* stone

*Piper - homeless girl, pipe player, *Joy* stone

*Quicksilver - medical, financial ID, GPS biochip

Samuel - one of the six captains, peacemaker

Sanctuary - the underground Eden-like forest

*Son of Chayeem - sprouted from the seed of Chayeem

*Tanahiel - another young woman, *Sanctuary* stone

*Teedhar - Todah's guardian angel, bringer of the *Dawn* stone

*Thummim - the stone of *Truths*

*Todah - a plain young woman, *Dawn* stone

*Tri-World Church - Triparteum's recognized religion

*Triparteum - the new one-world government

*Urim - the stone of *Lights,* Revelation

*Zek - Anna's guardian angel

*Zemir - an angel, Kate's friend (sword Hashamayeem, *Heaven* stone)

Prologue

(Recap)

The world grew darker, more evil by the day, and chaos spread. In order to combat this, government, economic, and religious societies came together to form a one-world government called the Triparteum. After chancellor Adonis Ashereem had brought peace to the Middle East and had miraculously recovered from a fatal assassination attempt, the people began to call him the savior of the world and eventually to worship and pray to him as the head of the Tri-World Church. In order to buy, sell, or do any business in this new world order you needed to possess Quicksilver. This bioelectronic chip, implanted in your wrist or in a tattoo on your forehead if you were a Quicksilver fanatic, contained all your personal, medical, and financial information. It also functioned as a GPS device. The Triparteum could determine your location anywhere on the planet and in real time. Having the chip began as a voluntary program, but soon became mandatory. Some people rebelled against the chip and the other demands of the society.

One group of dissidents had withdrawn from the city to a farm in the country. Many of them had felt led to the farm in obedience to specific direction from God. They formed their own religious society apart from the Tri-World Church, worshipping and following the God of the ancient Hebrew and Christian Scriptures. They had come from all walks of life, many from a local traveling circus, to populate this small, self-sustaining community that no longer needed to rely on the State for its survival or existence. The Triparterum initially tolerated them then subtly persecuted them through taxation, and, finally, openly attacked and destroyed them or at least thought they did.

A number of individuals at the farm had each been gifted, unbeknownst to each other, an ancient stone of divine origin. These gems had individual special characteristics that seemed to enhance their possessor's God given gifts, talents, and abilities. One young, blind girl, named Anna, was even able to see, albeit spiritually, through the possession of her stone. Another young man, a dwarf named Logan, had found a stone that enhanced his ability to communicate with animals. All of these stones were revealed after their pastor, Jon, accidentally discovered the lost Ark of the Covenant and after three of their younger members, Anna, Logan, and Tanahiel, had been led to a place called the Sanctuary while on a picnic. The Sanctuary was an underground forest of awe and wonder whose location was guarded and protected by an ancient centaur, Alathos, and some visible angels. The three young people led the farm's inhabitants to the Sanctuary shortly before the Triparteum destroyed the farm.

At the Sanctuary they met more stone-bearers as well as others who had been led there. They also met a wondrous talking tree, the Son of Chayeem. The original Chayeem, the Tree of Life, was found in the center of the garden of Eden. One of His seeds had been carried to the Sanctuary by Alathos many years earlier and planted in its garden. The Son of Chayeem spoke with the authority of God Himself and was the wisest being in the Sanctuary's garden just as his father was in the Garden of Eden.

PART 1 - RECOVERY

Chapter 1 - Is This Hell?

Just when you think you have things all figured out, life throws you a curve ball. Sometimes life becomes worse. Usually it becomes much better. But when one door slams closed in your face, another quietly opens behind you. It might help if you turn around.

From the "Musings of a Friend"

It was dark, so very dark. Julius held his hand up in front of his face, but could not see it. The explosion, if that was what it was, had been deafening and he still could not hear anything. He thought the entrance to the cave had collapsed, but he was unsure. "I am in hell, alone, and in utter darkness. Maybe, I am dead," he thought. Then someone bumped into him. Suddenly, there was light, not flaming sword light, but the translucent light of a glowing sword, giving off enough light for them all to see for a few cubits around them. Zek stood, his sword drawn. Aaron also stood, his staff giving off a light blue glow from the crystal atop it, which Alathos had given him. Anna had been thrown from Alathos' back by the concussion of the explosion, but, miraculously, onto the only patch of grass nearby. She got to her knees.

Alathos regained his footing and addressed her, " Anna, can you see what happened?"

In an almost prayer-like attitude she responded from her knees, "Ben, the false angel, spoke and used the sound of his voice as a weapon against us, creating an explosion. The blast threw us back far enough into the cave that when the entrance collapsed we were unharmed, but Teedhar and Mary were destroyed."

Alathos probed further, "Anything else?"

She continued, "It seems as though they think we were all killed in the blast and subsequent collapse of the entrance. They have retreated triumphantly."

Jon had been staggering to his feet when he heard Anna state that Mary had been destroyed. He collapsed back to his knees and whimpered at Anna, "Mary, dead again? She can't be! How can you be certain? You no longer wear the Way Stone," he cried.

"I'm sorry, Jon, but it's true. She perished in the blast with Teedhar," she spoke just above a whisper. "God gave me this sight when He gave me the Way Stone. When I gave the stone back to Him he let me keep His gift. I'm so sorry, but she's gone."

Jon began to weep uncontrollably. This was different than losing her to a brain aneurysm. Now he had lost her to the enemy. Little Logan stepped from behind a rock. They had almost forgotten that he and the hawk Dal had also been with them. He placed his hand on the kneeling Jon and emitted the sound of shared pain like the whimpering of a hurt animal. Then he embraced Jon, and when he did, it was like he sucked all the grief out of Jon's heart. Jon abruptly quit crying. He looked up at Logan and, as the beginnings of a smile began to grace his lips, leaned in and kissed him lightly on the forehead.

"Thank you, Logan, I needed that," he said simply.

Logan turned his attention to Anna, "Dal took wing just before the explosion. Did he escape?"

Anna dipped her head again, "Yes, he did. They tried to shoot him out of the sky, and they think that they succeeded, but he was only pretending to be hit. I lost sight of him as he fell into the trees, but I believe that he is all right."

Zek handed his sword to Jon and lifted Anna onto Alathos' back again.

Aaron turned to face Alathos, "What are we going to do now? The Triparteum has destroyed the entrance to the Sanctuary," he said with obvious concern.

Alathos smiled, "And what makes you think this was the only way in and out of the Sanctuary?"

Chapter 2 - Repercussions

*The days are coming when it seems that evil abounds
on all sides and darkness prevails on all fronts,
but we see what cannot be seen by mortal eyes and
are comforted in the unexpected and the seemingly
insignificant.*

From the "Stone Tablets of Ur"

By the time the troupe returned, the village already buzzed with questions. The concussion and shockwave of the explosion had shaken the Sanctuary. Many thought it an earthquake and they feared they were about to be buried alive. Most had no idea what had happened, but were nonetheless filled with fear. Their peaceful and idealistic existence had suddenly been shattered. The multitude congregated near the Pillar of Fire as Aaron, with the bruised and battered others, straggled into their midst.

A cacophony of voices asked some version of the same question, "What happened?"

Aaron regained his regal bearing as he stood tall and responded, "The Triparteum attacked us at the entrance to the Sanctuary. Mary and the angel Teedhar have been destroyed and the entrance collapsed. The explosion knocked the rest of us back into the tunnel and we barely escaped with our lives.

The barrage of questions continued, "Are we trapped in here then?"

Alathos stepped forward, Anna still on his back, "No, that was not the only entrance to this place. While it was the only obvious entrance, there are others."

Anna sat up straighter on Alathos' back and elaborated, "The Triparteum's army led by the false angel Ben, son of Adonis, attacked us at the entrance. They currently believe they have destroyed us all, but that will prove an incorrect assumption when our exploits back into the city resume."

The calm assurance that God was still in control and that this was, after all, His Sanctuary slowly replaced the fear and panic.

Suddenly, His voice echoed from the Pillar of Fire into each heart. "This is only the beginning of much tribulation, the likes of which the world has never seen before, but remember I have overcome the world. The world's version of death only releases you into a greater life with Me. Please, return back to your homes and suppers. Tomorrow we begin preparation for our greatest invasion back into the world. Aaron, José, and Meshar, would you please remain with me and enter the Pillar of Fire?"

With God's words ringing in their hearts the congregation turned and, in small groups of twos and threes, departed to their respective homes and to the cooking facilities to begin preparation for supper. Aaron, José, and Meshar entered the Pillar of Fire.

Although a somewhat common occurrence for them, it was still far from ordinary to walk into and through the Pillar of Fire. The atmosphere of holy awe inside it took your breath away each time you entered. The Ark, God's palpable presence, the two covering cherubim, the Tree, these would always make this place special and unique.

God spoke, "The unholy trinity of Adonis, Baalel, and Ben Ha-Chiya-Ra, doubles its efforts to destroy the elect, but I have heard the prayers of the martyrs and will answer. I will begin to bring My judgments on the world. In these next few critical weeks we will draw all those who will repent to join us here in My Sanctuary. Tomorrow, I want you to begin a special outpouring of My gifts to the congregation. You know that the weapons of our warfare differ from the world's weapons. My Holy Spirit will especially empower to accomplish what these last days need. The time is short, and the enemy knows that. To that end, in the morning the Tree will have moved out of my Pillar. Only a few have had the courage to meet Me in this place, but many will find it easier to meet me at the Tree until they truly learn we can communicate with one another at any time and in any place. Do you have any questions?" They felt no need to voice any, so they just looked at one another and shook their heads.

"Good," He continued, "and, as you already know, I am always with you."

They turned together and left the Pillar of Fire and His physical presence. Meanwhile, Todah came running up to Jon.

"Jon," she cried, "I just heard the news. Mary and Teedhar were killed in an attack on the entrance to the Sanctuary?"

"Yes, I am afraid so," said Jon, "The false angel Ben lied to Mary. She was disconsolate after the birth of Julius and Judy's child and wandered out of the entrance. The angel met her there and told her that he could give her a son if she went back in and brought me out to meet him. She did, but he did not realize that she would bring others with her. He attacked us and, just before he did, Teedhar stepped in front to shield me. He saved my life, but at the sacrifice of his own."

Todah began to weep uncontrollably and fell to her knees to grasp Jon around his knees. He bent over and held her to him until she was only sobbing.

"I am sorry Todah, I know how much he meant to you," Jon whispered into her hair.

"But he's been with me my whole life," she whimpered, "it's not fair!" Suddenly it looked like she was working up a head of steam towards anger.

Jon tried to figure out how to stop her train of thought. He countered gently, "And I have lost Mary for the second time." That seemed to derail her for the moment.

"I'm sorry, Jon, how inconsiderate of me." She had a bit of her normal composure back. "Your loss is surely as deep as mine." They held each other a while longer, then Jon helped her to her feet.

"We need to go talk to the Tree," he said and headed off in its direction, still holding her by the hand.

"But Jon," she stammered, "it's engulfed within the Pillar of Fire."

"I know," he said authoritatively and continued at a brisk pace. When they reached the pillar, he did not even hesitate, but walked right in, pulling her in with him. The two angels, one at each end of the Ark, drew their flaming swords and a voice thundered out of the Tree.

"It takes a great deal of courage, Jon, to enter the pillar unbidden," said the Tree, "you are either very courageous or very foolish today."

Jon realized that his grief had gotten the better of him. He fell to one knee before the Tree, again dragging Todah down with him. "I meant no disrespect, Sir."

"And you have brought young Todah with you, she is one of my favorites," He said.

Todah found her voice then, "My Lord, Mary and Teedhar have been destroyed in an attack on the Sanctuary!"

The voice interrupted her, "And you think this has escaped my notice?" The thunder of His voice receded into a chuckle.

"No, Sir," she stopped mid sentence, "you're right. Our grief has made us foolish."

The voice interrupted again, "Teedhar was not destroyed. He is right here." Teedhar stepped from behind the Ark and walked under the branches of the Tree. "Angels are not mortal like humans. They cannot be destroyed, certainly not by the false angel Ben Ha-Chiya-Ra. Angels are immortal and Teedhar is fine. I was just thanking him for protecting Jon and was preparing to return him to you or you to him, to bring the two of you back together. Thank you, by the way, for lending him to block the assault on this place."

But Todah hardly listened. She had jumped up and run to Teedhar's arms and wept for sheer joy.

The Tree continued, "And you, Jon, know that Mary is not dead. She has just lost the use of that body. The Gideonite had corrupted it anyway."

After Mary's first death by a brain aneurysm, she had been resurrected by the Triparteum scientist, Doctor Gideon Anakim, through use of his discovery. Gideonite was found in a meteor and used to replace the damaged portions of her brain and also to create the brain that housed the artificial intelligence that gave the false angel Ben Ha-Chiya-Ra his life. The link between the two portions of Gideonite had betrayed the location of the

Sanctuary's entrance and provided the opportunity for the attack.

"Unfortunately," the Tree began again, "you will have to wait until after the Great Resurrection to be physically reunited with her, but she is with me and, therefore, is a party to all that is going on here."

"Yes," Jon responded as he sighed deeply, "and thank you for taking care of her, as well as reuniting Todah and Teedhar." Jon stood, and the three of them turned to go.

The Tree spoke again. "Jon." Jon turned back, "Never forget how fond I am of you."

Chapter 3 - Reinvigoration

The good things in life are worth the work required to achieve them. They are worth the blood, sweat, and tears it takes to produce them, but it was not always like that. It used to be easier, simpler, when everything and everyone cooperated with everything and everyone else, and that time will come once again. Help us return to that simpler life...

From the "Simple Book of Returning"

The next morning word rapidly rippled through the entire congregation, "The Tree no longer stands inside the Pillar of Fire. It now stands rooted in front of it and provides easy access for all of us to its physical representation of God Himself." Although some had entered the Pillar of Fire to talk with God and had returned unscathed, it had never been intended to separate the people into those who had and those who had not. Still, a subconscious feeling pervaded that some people were more special than others. That feeling evaporated completely with open access to the Tree for everyone.

After breakfast the entire congregation, about six hundred strong, met before the Tree which now stood in front of the Pillar of Fire. The Tree had grown taller than the full height of a man. You could now walk unhindered beneath it branches. Aaron stood next to the Tree, his hand casually grasping one of His lower branches.

The Son of Chayeem spoke, "Thank you for coming this morning. As you know, I have a personal relationship with each of you, but something special, something more, happens when we are gathered together." For no obvious reason everyone who could kneel did. It was simply a sign of respect for the Tree.

The Tree continued, "Today begins a time of strategic training for the days ahead. We need to prepare for the days of trouble, which are descending upon the whole world. I am going to judge the world for its rebellion and wrong. You are each called to be in the world, but not to be a part of it. Some will still change their hearts, minds, and ways and begin to join us. We are to call them to this change and lead them back here that they too may be equipped to participate in this final harvest. To expedite and accomplish this I need to call forth six captains, one for each one hundred of you. These six are no different than you, for you will each be uniquely gifted to participate in this endeavorer. As I call you will you please join Aaron here beneath my branches?"

The Tree called forth the men Eleazar and Samuel, the angels Meezimore and Mishal, (who were currently standing there in their human form), and the animals Kate (the pelican) and Azinath (the great eagle). Aaron gave each of them a bowl of water from the spring and a censer.

"Please have the congregation stand. I would like each of you leaders to sprinkle the hundred that you represent with the water from the spring," said Chayeem, "as a sign of purification and consecration to the tasks ahead of us."

The two men and the two angels took their bowls in one hand and censers in the other, dipped their censers in their bowls and and began to sprinkle those they represented as they walked among them. Kate and Azinath's task was somewhat easier. They took their censers in their beaks, dipped them in the bowls, and then flew over their people, sprinkling them as they went. They occasionally flew back to their bowls to replenish their censers and then continued to sprinkle their people. When the two birds were finished, they returned to the Tree and perched within its branches. The others continued until the purification and consecration of their people were complete, then they too returned to stand beneath the branches of the Tree with Aaron.

Chayeem spoke again, "Have the congregation relax on the ground as best they can." They gestured to the congregation, and they did so.

"I am now going to move among them and distribute my gifts to them." Suddenly, the Pillar of Fire that stood behind the Tree changed in appearance. Where it had been a simple pillar of fire that rose from the ground to the sky, it began to rotate and whirl. The fire then spread out, over and above the heads of the congregation. As it did so, everyone, men, angels, and animals, toppled over where they sat. It was as if suddenly they all just fell asleep. The two birds had come down from the branches of the Tree to sit on the ground. Then all of the leaders too collapsed to the ground, including Aaron.

After a few minutes individuals began to awaken, appearing refreshed and invigorated. Aaron had them all stand once again, Todah led them in a song of worship and praise, and they dismissed them to their day's normal tasks until lunch. The six, appointed leaders remained with Aaron for further instruction.

PART 2 -
MY WITNESS

Chapter 4 - Hiding Until…

Why do I hide a thing?

Some things are hidden to age and become more flavorful; others because they are too precious to be seen by all, and still others are hidden until the time is ripe for them to be revealed.

From the "Book of Secrets"

Dal and the old man, with the child still sleeping on his back, continued their journey for the better part of the day without interruption except for an occasional stop for water. The old man's stamina was amazing. Dal flew reconnaissance above the forest, so had the easier journey. Hash (short for Hashadiel), Judy and Julius' son, finally woke up full of questions. The old man placed him on the ground to walk beside him. They seemed to be following some kind of game trail, so while the traveling was rocky, it was not particularly difficultly for the man and the boy. Hash politely addressed the old man as "Grandfather."

"Grandfather, where are we?"

"We are still in the forest beyond the hills which contain the Sanctuary," the old man replied.

"And where are we going?" Hash asked.

"Well, when Alathos and I spoke with the Tree this morning, He said that we had to leave the Sanctuary quickly. He told us of a place to the north in the forests where we could hide for a time," the man answered.

"Why do we need to hide, and why did Alathos not come with us, Grandfather?" the boy continued.

"Well, son, look at the terrain. While you and I can traverse these rocks fairly easily, it would be more difficult for a centaur, and he is the guardian of the Sanctuary," said the old man.

"But, I miss him Grandfather. I like him quite a lot," mused the boy.

"Yes, I think we all like Alathos quite a lot."

"You didn't say why we need to hide," Hash repeated.

"Hmm, that requires some explanation," smiled the man, "and we seem to have the time now, do we not?" He spoke softly to himself, "And it will make the journey go more quickly."

"Ok, I am listening," the boy smiled too.

"Where to start, where to start," the old man said to himself. "Hash, you have grown up in the Sanctuary your entire life. What do you know about the Triparteum?"

"They are our enemy or, at least, they work for our enemy, but we are not to hate them. I am to love them, pray for them, and if I ever meet them, have compassion and mercy on them." Hash had obviously internalized some important lessons for one so young.

The old man's smile deepened in appreciation at the answer. "Unfortunately, they do not like us at all. Because we follow the Liberator, they are forever hunting us down and trying to destroy us. That is why we had to leave and must hide. The Triparteum has attacked the Sanctuary and believe they have destroyed it. If they knew where we were, they would attack us also."

Hash's smile quickly turned upside-down. "But, Grandfather, they cannot destroy the Sanctuary. God is there, with His Ark, His Tree, His Pillar of Fire."

The man's smile dimmed too. "That is true, but they attacked it, nonetheless, and some have died."

Concern swept over the boy's face. "Who, Grandfather? Who has died?"

"I am not sure, son, but I believe we have lost some of our friends, at least for the time being, but in the end, all will be made right." His smile returned a little.

Just then they emerged from the rocks into a small meadow and found Dal standing on a large rock off to the side of the game trail, now more visible before them.

"I think I have found it," he said, although it was difficult to tell if he spoke to the old man, the boy, or to both.

"Good," replied the man, "we will soon be out of daylight."

"I will continue to scout ahead." Dal launched himself into flight about 4 cubits off the ground.

The old man and the boy followed in his direction, out of the meadow, into the forest, to discover a small mountain stream. The trail continued beside it and so did they, until they rounded a corner and came face to face with the opening of a cave.

"It's another Sanctuary!" exclaimed the lad.

"It does seem rather coincidental," added the old man as the three of them entered it. This cave, however, was not a tunnel into another underground forest, but widened into a rather large cavern just before the daylight ran out. The old man reached back into one of the pockets in his pack, retrieving a large jewel that soon began to glow quite brightly.

Hash exclaimed excitedly, "Grandfather, you have one of the stones of fire!"

The old man responded, "While not one of the twelve stones of judgment that were assembled to ignite the pillar of fire, Alathos did lend me this stone for our travels. I think it is as mysterious in its origin as the green peridot that was given to Meshar. He did not offer me any explanation, only that he thought it might be useful." The old man did not mention that Alathos had also told him that the stone would lead to a second stone which would one day be Hash's when the time was appropriate. He placed the stone on a nearby ledge and suddenly the entire cavern brightened as the crystal ceiling within it caught and reflected the light of the jewel. The cavern felt unusually warm when they followed Dal around a corner as he continued to scout. Beyond the curve they discovered a series of hot springs. All they needed now was an ample source of food, and they would be able to stay in the cavern indefinitely. The crystal light followed them around another corner where a thick layer of what looked like moss covered the ground. Grandfather bent down and touched it.

"Hmm," he muttered, "moss is usually wet, but this is not." The air, while still warm, was no longer as humid.

"I think this will be a great place to stay," said the old man.

"And to explore," said the boy. With that Dal fluttered back and landed beside them both.

"You will not believe what is around the next bend. It is like an entire mushroom garden," he exclaimed, awestruck.

Chapter 5 - The First Witness

…and I will give authority and power to my two witnesses. They are like the two trees standing in My presence. When they speak, even death will listen spellbound. Though the enemy will come against them, he will be unable to harm them. Rather, armies will be slain by their words. When they speak, the heavens will close, and all the plagues of the enemy will be turned back against his armies. They will stand unharmed, invincible, until they have spoken the full measure of their words.

From the "Words of Chayeem"

They could not call it the Sanctuary, since they had come from there. Calling it the second Sanctuary did not seem right either without the Tree, the Ark, or the Pillar of Fire. They finally settled on calling it simply their Headquarters, HQ for short. While it proved to be an amazing place, it paled in comparison to the Sanctuary. It did have the crystal roof that captured and reflected the light from the stone that Grandfather brought with them. It had the hot springs that provided warmth and a great bathing experience, wonderfully dry moss to sleep on, and the mushroom garden. Somehow it was superbly ventilated. They could build a small fire to cook with and the smoke just drifted up and dissipated. It never smelled smoky, nor did their clothing.

Dal, Hash, and Grandfather sat around their small cooking fire, Dal gnawing on the remains of something. It seemed incongruous for him to eat meat even outside of the Sanctuary, but whatever he ate he seemed to thoroughly enjoy. Hash and Grandfather ate their evening variation of the morning's mash. Its contents depended on what they had been able to forage that day. Grandfather was teaching Hash all the intricacies of a woodsman's skills. The training probably mimicked how Bahn trained a young pastor Jon many years earlier, at least, according to the rumors. Grandfather called them the Six S's: sanctity, safety, simplicity, silence or stealth, sufficiency of self, and sacrifice. Shortly after they had arrived at the HQ they had taken apart the pack that Grandfather had brought with him from the Sanctuary and sewn it into two small daypacks, one for each of them. In these they carried a light lunch and whatever hand tools they might need that day. They had made most of the hand tools themselves. The two of them spent this particular morning practicing stealth, seeing how closely they could creep up on a wild animal before being discovered. They only got a "point" if they actually tagged the animal, and they tried to do it in such a way that they did not frighten them. They intended no harm. That was the first "S"; the sanctity of life, all life.

Grandfather had initially been surprised that Hash could still understand Dal when he spoke. In the Sanctuary everyone understood everyone else—men, animals, and angels, because each evening they all ate of the fruit of the Tree Chayeem. Out here in the HQ, they no longer had access to His fruit, yet they could still all understand one another. At first, Grandfather thought the fruit might have had some cumulative effect or that Hash, like Logan, had been given the gift of understanding the animals. Perhaps it stayed with him because Hash had grown up always being able to understand everyone and had never known anything less. Therefore, Grandfather had to make a rule that convincing the animals to allow themselves to be tagged violated the purpose of learning stealth. Hash could only befriend them after tagging them. They had played the stealth game long enough that Hash had befriended most of the animals in their immediate neighborhood, so their adventures had to take place further and further away to truly test Hash's skills. As a side benefit to having a neighborhood of animal friends, no one could sneak up on the HQ. Someone would report any enemy who tried. It enhanced the level of sanctity and safety growing around the HQ, but also posed another problem.

Once you met Hash and became his friend, you just liked being around him. Animals tended to congregate around them whenever and wherever they traveled, which made it difficult for them to remain unnoticed. Hash finally needed to convince the animals that sometimes he should be left alone. He did so diplomatically, without hurting anyone's feelings. When they needed to travel alone, he wore his coonskin cap. They had found the dead coon one day during an attempt to travel alone. They were not sure of the cause of its death, but they took it back to the HQ, skinned it, buried the remains with a bit of ceremony, tanned the hide and made a cap from it. All Hash's animal friends knew the story and were not offended that he wore the cap. It became their signal to allow him space to travel stealthily without the normal entourage.

One evening while they sat around the fire eating their supper, Grandfather asked Hash, "Do you know what your name means?"

Hash responded, "My parents always told me I was special, destined for a unique purpose, but I don't recall that they ever told me exactly what my name meant."

Grandfather continued, "It means The Witness of God. The Son of Chayeem reminded us, after you were born, that in these last days there would be two witnesses that stand against the evil armies of an evil age. I believe that you are one of the two."

The boy stammered, "Is this a good thing? I mean, how can I stand against the armies of the Triparteum? I am just a boy!"

"Remember, three young people led your parents to the Sanctuary in the first place, and you are the offspring of that same place of awe and wonder," Grandfather encouraged.

"Yeah, but they each had one of the Stones of Fire. What do I have?" Hash countered.

Grandfather frowned a bit, "You know as well as I do that the stones are not magic. They are simply gifts with a purpose."

Hash remained unconvinced, "And what gifts do I have?"

Grandfather hoped to increase the boy's faith, "Wasn't your mother healed when in the hospital?"

"Yes," he said sheepishly.

"And did she not also later regain her lost sight?" Grandfather seemed to be building up to something.

"Yes, she did."

"And did not your father use humor and illusion to bring hope to the kids at the children's hospital?"

"So I have been told."

"Then perhaps you have gifts that you have not experienced yet." There, he had said it.

Like he had finally flipped a switch, the boy's doubts gave way to his faith and hope that began in his eyes and spread across his face.

"And you will help me find them, Grandfather?" He was not pleading; he was closer to stating a fact.

"Yes, son, I will." They both breathed a sigh of relief and went on to speak of things of lesser consequence. Dal had been standing by silently, but with a wink he began telling the story of his own vision quest and his finding of the Night stone. Hash's smile increased. Maybe a special stone waited in his future, otherwise why would Dal tell that story?

PART 3 - PREPARATION

Chapter 6 - Beginning Preparations

Soldier: When will I be ready to fight the enemy?

Master: When you have mastered the seven: confidence, intention, pressure, opportunity, fullness, and sacrifice.

Soldier: But, Master, you have only named six. Master: Well, at least you can count.

From the "Master's Strategies of Engagement"

The Pillar of Fire had returned to normal, as normal as a pillar of fire could be. Eleazar, Samuel, Meezimore, Mishal, Kate, and Azinath stood before the Tree with Aaron after the others had departed. Sometimes, they did not know how to behave in front of the Tree. Should they kneel, bow, or, in this case, just stand there in response to His request?

The Son of Chayeem spoke, "As I was saying, we will be strategically increasing our preparation and training for a series of enhanced exploits back into the world, in order to call as many as possible to change their hearts and come back here with you. They will only be able to enter this place if their hearts have been changed, so you need not worry about being infiltrated by enemy spies. I have just distributed seven major categories of gifts to the congregation. These gifts are the weapons we will use to offensively attack the gates of hell. As I call them out, one by one, you will feel the gift rising in your heart confirming your possession of it. When that happens, please take a step forward."

They all nodded their understanding and assent.

The Tree began, "Proclamation of the Truth." Azinath stepped forward.

The Tree continued, "Peacemaking." Samuel stepped forward and the Tree added, "you will be joining Meshar with that gift."

He then said, "Worship," and Meezimore stepped forward. "You will join Todah, Piper, and José with this same gifting."

"There are two hospitality gifts," said the Tree, "Feeding the hungry is the first." Eleazar stepped forward. "Julius and Judy will help you with that gift. The second is clothing the naked." Kate hopped forward. "You will join Logan and Tanaheil as you learn all that will be needed to express that gift. And whom do we have left? Ah, Mishal and Aaron, you thought I had forgotten you, but no. I have left the best for last. Mishal." He called out.

And Mishal stepped forward. "I believe that your heart resonates with prayer! While each of you and your gifts are very important, all that we are and do must be covered and connected by prayer."

"Mishal," the Tree went on, "as you know, prayer is just talking to me, even when you are not standing in front of me; and listening to me, even when you are not before me. That is how simple prayer is meant to be, a conversation. However, as an angel, you also know that prayer is the foundation of everything that is accomplished, and that nothing is accomplished unless it is spoken into being through prayer. Prayer is the lubricant that keeps everything running and also the fuel that everything needs in order to run. You, Mishal, will lead our prayer warriors."

Aaron stepped forward and knelt before the tree. "And for me, Lord?" he questioned.

"Ah, Aaron," responded the Tree, "we both know what is near and dear to your heart. Besides joining Azinath in the proclamation of the good news, you will be joining my two witnesses in the demonstration of signs and wonders, especially in healing and deliverance."

"Your two witnesses, Sir?" Aaron also asked.

"That, my friend, is a topic for another time. If you all would, please gather around my trunk. Men and angels hold hands, and angels touch wings with the birds." They did so. "Now." He spoke and they all collapsed on the ground again. "Hmm, perhaps it will be easier this way?" whispered the Tree. "I will just share the plan with them while they rest in the glory of my presence."

As they lay there, Chayeem shared with them, "After lunch, I will have the congregation reassemble. I will then call forth those with the same gift that each of you possess, have you move to a specific location separate from each other, and begin training those who have followed you in how to use their gift. The actual composition of each exploit team I will share at a later time."

They began to awaken, stand, and realize they had received their instructions. Chayeem dismissed them to their lunches as well.

After lunch the congregation reassembled, sat on the ground, and, as Chayeem introduced each of the leaders and their gift, those with that gift stood up and followed their leader to the place their leader had chosen.

Chapter 7 -
The Weapon of Peace

Blessed are the peacemakers
for they shall be called sons of God.

Matthew 5:9

That afternoon Samuel and about 60 others, a mix of men, women, animals, and angels, gathered around Meshar in the center of the practice field. The humans and the angels took a knee out of respect. The animals took other postures that signified their focused attention.

He addressed them reverently; "We have all been called to a sacred duty and gifted in a unique way to help accomplish the task of calling people to repentance from the ways of the world. The goal is a change of heart that will allow them to follow us back to this place. How many of you are familiar with my story?"

A majority of appendages were raised. "Then I will be brief in retelling it," he said. "I trained from my youth as a soldier and warrior. I was very good at it. When the Triparteum's military arm was established, I was conscripted into it. I was given additional training to develop what they thought was the psychic side of my personality. What they did not realize was by enhancing my spiritual sensitivity, they were helping me see not only their dark side of things, but also to be open to the light. How many of you are also familiar with the martial arts?"

Fewer responded to that question.

He continued, "Well, those of us who are fully trained in the martial arts realize that they are more art than martial. Our ability to excel in the art is attributed less to our physical training, although that is important, and more to development of the right character. Because my heart was set on justice, I was also able to learn mercy. Because I sought the truth, I was able to discern falsehood. Though initially fighting for the enemy, I was left wounded and defeated on the doorstep to the Sanctuary in order to find my true calling. I then had to empty myself of all my initial learning and relearn a multitude of things to become a different kind of warrior. In the end I was finally trained with one of the singing swords that was a remnant of the Hail'yk. Eventually, I was entrusted with the stone of Peace it contained. That stone now forms a part of the circle enshrining the Pillar of Fire. My name is Meshar, meaning Peace, and I was given the stone of Peace. I learned how to use peace as a weapon, to become a peacemaker. It is now my task to teach this to you."

The young man Cephas raised his hand. Meshar acknowledged it.

"Master Meshar, how are we to use peace as a weapon? That seems like a contradiction of terms," Cephas asked.

"You do not need to call me master. We have only one master here," Meshar responded. "Your name is Cephas, meaning pebble, but a stone has many uses. In a stream, with others, it purifies water. In a tumbler it helps to polish others. In a sling it becomes a projectile. Finally, in a mill, it grinds our wheat. A stone is just a stone until it is used. So it will be with you and peace," he took a deep breath and said, "You have each been given a gift of peace. You must now learn how to use that gift."

Meshar spoke in a loud, commanding voice, "We have all had problems with someone, even here in the Sanctuary. Look around you and see if any of the people you have had a problem with are a part of our group."

Inhabitants of the Sanctuary made no distinction between humans, angels, and animals, treating each as having the same inherent value, yet the variety of differences could cause problems. Though a wonderful place of peace and safety, conflicts arose naturally all the time. Because everyone genuinely cared about everyone else, they dealt with their own problems as they arose. Still, differences in gender (except in the angels), in personality, in skills, in functions, in maturity, all contained potential to breed conflict.

Meshar then demonstrated the first lesson he had for his peacemakers. As everyone was looking around, Meshar walked over and stood by Jordan, a tall man of athletic build and somewhat military bearing.

Meshar continued, "Jordan, here, came to us recently and, like myself, had been enlisted in the Triparteum's army prior to coming here. He was in their infantry, where I was in special branch and black ops, so we had not met before he turned up on our doorstep." He said this in a rather condescending manner that was unusual for Meshar, but he was doing it on purpose and for a purpose. "Jordan reports to me and is still in the process of unlearning his old military behavior and replacing it with what I am trying to teach him. Before he joined us, he had attained the rank of colonel and was used to men following his orders without question. Here we are rank-less and do not order each other around. Because that is so different from his prior experience, he has often found it difficult."

While Meshar described Jordan and the situation, Jordan visibly began to bristle.

Meshar produced a broom, seemingly out of thin air and held it out to Jordan. "Jordan, if I told you right now to go sweep out the kitchen, what would be your response?"

By now on the verge of open anger, Jordan grabbed the broom and growled through clenched teeth, "I would politely tell you where you could stick your broom. In fact, perhaps not very politely."

The angel Manasseh stepped forward. From somewhere, he had produced his own broom and addressed Jordan. "I would be honored to sweep the kitchen with you Jordan. May I?" Amazingly, as if Manasseh had pricked the balloon of Jordan's pent up anger it was gone.

Jordan replied, as his frown slowly morphed into a smile, "I would like that, Manasseh. I would like that a lot. Let's go sweep the kitchen."

The tension that had built up and affected all of them almost completely dissipated in that instant, and many faces now held the trace of their own growing smile.

Meshar addressed the entire group again, "Do you see how a simple word or action can defuse an entire situation and bring peace? Manasseh did just that by offering to join Jordan in the task he found so distasteful." He addressed Manasseh, "How did you know what to do, Manasseh? How did you know to grab a broom and offer to join Jordan in sweeping the kitchen?"

Manasseh replied, "I felt a prompting in my heart to do so, and it seemed like something the Son of Chayeem might ask me to do for someone else."

"Ah....," mused Meshar, "this is the key to the use of your gift. Listen to your heart, to your spirit. The Tree is always with us and He will help guide us in the practical use of this gift. It is not enough to want to bring peace, not enough to know that I have been gifted to bring peace, even the *how* is up to Him."

Manasseh seemed to interrupt Meshar, but that was because he was still listening to Chayeem. "I also quickly knew that how I asked him was also very important. I needed to convey to him that I would be honored to join him in the task."

"Yes," added Jordan, "how he asked to help me made all the difference."

Meshar addressed the group again, "So, pair up with someone you have had difficulty with in the past. Those of you who are left, join a pair as its third party." He watched them as they complied. In many cases the third part of a group was an angel. He spoke again, "You will notice that in many of your groups of three the third party is an angel, just as it was Manasseh who intervened in our example. Angels do not generally have the problems or conflicts with people or animals that we do. They can, but they are much less selfish than the rest of us and are more accustomed to serving. You will also find that their ability to hear Chayeem is more developed, but all of this can be improved with practice. That is why we are here. So, go ahead, create a conflict between the two of you, and watch the third party act as a peacemaker."

Although they all wanted to learn how to be peacemakers it was more difficult for some of the trios to create a conflict situation even when the person was someone with whom they had a prior conflict. As Meshar walked around, he watched the individual trios practicing and interrupted one that was having particular trouble.

"Todd," asked Meshar, "what seems to be the problem?"

"Well," responded Todd, somewhat reluctantly, "Samuel and I have had difficulty in the past, so we decided to try this on each other, but he's a leader now and it just doesn't seem right to pick a fight with him. It doesn't seem right."

Samuel added, "I told him it was OK, but that didn't seem to help."

"Hmmm," Meshar mused, "Did you ask Chayeem?"

Todd bristled a little, "Ask Him what!"

"If it was OK to pick a fight with Samuel." Meshar was smiling now.

He bristled more, "No, I didn't ask Chayeem if I could pick a fight with Samuel, but you seem pretty proficient at picking a fight with me!" Now he was steaming.

Cephas stepped in, "Todd, would it help if you picked it with me?"

That seemed to bring things down a notch.

"It might," conceded Todd.

"And we could ask Chayeem for permission before we start?" added Cephas.

"That would probably help too." Todd had almost returned to calm.

"Ah," the revelation was dawning for Todd as he said, "we are not just trying to learn a technique for making peace. We are learning to experience a greater interdependency with Chayeem. Rather than me trying to manufacture a situation, I needed to ask Him for help with all facets of the interaction. This is harder than it seems and at the same time simpler."

"Now you have it!" praised Meshar. "Before you switch roles, begin by asking Him who should be in each role. Then, ask what the conflict should be about and then how to resolve it. You have discovered the fundamental truth. It is all relational."

Meshar continued to walk around and beheld amazing progress. More trios were discovering the interdependent relational component of peacemaking. Even with offenses and conflicts that had occurred in the past, had been forgiven and worked through, when they were reviewed in the present they quickly brought back to the surface all the old feelings and emotions. It would have been easy for harsh words to be spoken, even for some fights to break out, but in each case, when the third party listened to Chayeem, they were able to step in and masterfully defuse the situation. Meshar had them regroup into other pairs and go through the process again, and again. They continued their practice until almost suppertime, when he dismissed them to freshen up before dinner.

Chapter 8 - Worship as a Weapon

Take everything about you, your entire being, all that you are, and all that you do, and give it to the Liberator daily as a continuous act of worship; not allowing the world to fashion you after its pattern, but as a part of an on-going process allowing yourself to be changed, letting His truth make your mind new.

Romans 12:1-2

In another part of the Sanctuary the angel Meezimore and humans Todah, Piper, and José gathered with about forty like-minded, like-gifted souls.

José addressed them, "We are gathered together as those who have been given the special gift of worship. Worship is not just about singing or music. We all know that worship is to characterize our entire lives; it is our style of living. However, we have been given worship in extra measure as a gift to be used in this next series of exploits. It is our goal, in these next few weeks, to have adequately demonstrated and participated in the use of worship as a strategic weapon on teams. Just as speaking with Chayeem can be done individually, there is something special that happens when two or three are gathered together to pray. Although it defies logic, when two or three are gathered in His name, He is somehow more present than when we are by ourselves. That is also true of worship."

He stopped to observe the crowd and found many nodding in assent.

José continued, "Meezimore, Todah, Piper, and I will each take a group of you off by ourselves and begin your training. Please number off one to four."

They began, with the first person saying "one," the next "two," then "three" and "four," and then began again with "one" until they had all been numbered.

"Now," José said, "number one folks follow Meezimore, number two folks Todah, threes with Piper and fours with me."

Each group took off in a different direction. José and his group walked a short distance to a small meadow that formed a natural amphitheater. They all sat on the ground; angels, humans, and animals, all that is, except Caleb the dog.

Caleb spoke, "Am I to assume that when we leave the Sanctuary we will also leave behind our ability to speak?"

José cocked his head to one side as if listening to someone. He did that because he was listening to Chayeem's answer to the question. He then responded, "The ability of us to all understand one another is unique to the Sanctuary and our participation in eating the fruit of the Tree. Outside of the Sanctuary we will all still be able to understand one another, but because the humans of the world have never been here or eaten of His fruit, they will not be able to understand you animals. I am sorry…but that may be a positive thing."

Caleb questioned, "How could that be a positive thing?"

José went on, "We are used to talking to you and understanding your response. Out in the world, hearing you talk would seem odd and unnatural. It might have a tendency to scare people."

Caleb replied, "So how are we to worship without using words?"

José smiled, "A wise man once said, 'Preach the gospel at all times and when necessary use words.' That probably also applies to worshipping while we are out there." He turned to the swallow Hasees. "Could you share with us the difference between a planned song and a spontaneous one?"

Hasees sang the verse and chorus of a worship song that they all knew by heart. Everyone felt the urge to join in. Then José had her sing it again and let everyone participate. After this she burst into spontaneous song, and it felt suddenly more mysterious, enchanting, captivating, and awe-inspiring all in one. It seemed as though the very atmosphere shifted, and spiritually it had.

José began again, "I think you all perceived that. As wonderful as the first song was that we all knew, the second song actually changed the spiritual atmosphere. That is true not only of song, but of each act of worship we perform while we are out with an exploit team. We will be in charge of changing the atmosphere and then maintaining that change until another one is required."

He turned to Caleb, "How might you help change the atmosphere?"

Caleb cocked his head to one side for a minute and then responded, "Most children inherently like dogs and, while they may not be familiar with friendly dogs, I can change that by the way I act towards them, wagging my tail, licking their hand, rubbing up against them."

"And those behaviors will change the atmosphere with the children, and that change will be infectious. It will spread to the adults as well," said José.

They continued in this way until José released them for supper.

PART 4 -
TIME IS SHORT

Chapter 9 - Another?

"And those on the earth and even in the sea should be very much afraid, for the enemy of your souls has come down from his home in the skies to you and he is very angry and in great haste, for he knows that his time is short!"

Revelation 12:12

(And the Liberator said) "Do not say, 'There are still four months until the harvest begins.' I tell you, 'The fields are ready for the harvest right now and the time is short!'"

John 4:35

Hash awoke and found that both Dal and Grandfather were gone. *"Hmmm,"* he pondered, *"something urgent must have required their attention."* He tidied up, splashed some water on his face, dried off, sat, and composed himself to wait. At times like this he especially missed the lush beauty of the forested Sanctuary. He continued to reminisce about the years he had spent there with his mom and dad and all their friends amidst the awe and wonder of the Pillar of Fire and the Tree. He did not feel sad, maybe a bit homesick, but mostly grateful. He had been blessed in the past and had no reason to doubt but that he would be equally blessed in the present and the future. The blessings would just be different.

He continued in this state until he heard the words whispered to his heart.

It sounded like the Tree speaking, "Are there parts of this cave that you have not explored?" Hash had never physically met the Tree. It had been engulfed in the Pillar of Fire shortly after his birth, but his parents had introduced him to the Tree spiritually when he was still very young.

"Yes," he responded to the Tree, "we have only gone this short way into the cave, just past the springs to this place where we have established our temporary home."

"Would you like to explore some more of it, rather than just waiting for them to return?" the Tree continued to whisper.

"Certainly, if that would be okay," Hash whispered back.

"Of course it would, and you know that I am always with you." Hash found it interesting how authoritative the Tree's whisper could be.

"Yes, Sir, I know that You are always with me and I assume so is my angel." Hash still whispered.

"Your angel?" questioned the Tree.

"My guardian angel, don't we each have a guardian angel?" asked Hash.

"Some need more than one," chuckled the Tree, "have you met yours?"

"I don't believe I have," Hash's anticipation was growing. "May I?"

"There were many angels in the Sanctuary, might not one of them been yours?" replied the Tree. "But then all of the angels there might not have been visible, eh?"

"I guess that I never really thought much about it," said Hash. "I think I was too busy just growing up. I did meet many of the visible angels. Was one of them my guardian?"

"No, none of the visible ones were yours," answered the Tree, "but I think it is time you met him. Ometz, would you please reveal yourself to Hashadiel." It was more of a command than a question.

Immediately before Hash stood a ten-foot tall angel complete in battle armor and sword. He would have been terrifying, except he smiled, and he had the kindest smile Hash had ever seen in his short but eventful life.

Ometz reached out his hand, "I am pleased to finally be allowed to meet you physically."

"Me, too." Hash reached out to shake his hand, but found that Ometz grasped his forearm instead. He tried to grasp Ometz' huge forearm, but not very successfully.

"Let me help you with that," the angel said as he shifted to his human form. He now appeared clad in normal attire, although still had his sword girded about his waist. The sword had shrunk in the same proportion that the angel had shrunk. "I think Chayeem wants us to explore this cave some more."

"Great, I'm not afraid of the dark, but I'll be even more brave with you by my side," Hash said over his shoulder as he walked away. "Thank you, Chayeem."

Together Hash and Ometz strode off towards the back of the cavern. As the light of the crystals began to fade, Ometz silently drew his sword. Hash was a bit disappointed. He had heard of the singing swords, but had yet to encounter one. Subconsciously he had hoped that his guardian angel might have one.

As though hearing Hash's thoughts, Ometz said, "Only seven singing swords were created and given to the archangels. Well, eight, since Alathos took the lost remains of Hail'yk and made it into two others. You know Meshar has one of those don't you?"

"He does?" exclaimed Hash, "Well, he keeps it a secret."

"Maybe he's keeping it hidden for a special time," said the angel, "though I think we may soon need all the help we can get."

"Yours isn't one of the flaming swords is it?" asked Hash, still a bit crestfallen.

"Hmm," said Ometz, "soon you're going to make me feel like just a normal, ordinary, run-of-the-mill angel."

"I'm sorry," apologized Hash, "I didn't mean to make you feel bad."

Ometz smile turned to laughter, "You did not make me feel bad, young one, I was just having a bit of fun at your questioning. You see, every created being is special and unique in its own way and things are often not what they seem at present. I am sure you have heard the stories of the stones of fire and how many of them were unrecognizable in their darkened state. Each of us is similar. We need to not just see each other for who we are right now, but believe that the Tree will help each of us walk into the fullness of our destiny."

"Yup," smiled Hash, "that's one of the drawbacks of being young. I'm not as wise as I should or could be."

"Ah, but you will be," countered the angel. "Now, back to our exploring."

They turned a corner in the cave and it enlarged substantially. Ometz's sword burst into light and the crystals in this part of the cavern did the same. Before them stood a huge Being of utter darkness. It seemed to consume the light around it, but Ometz's sword continued to supply even more light.

The Being spoken ominously, "You are frustrated in your attempts to give the child the stone!" It drew its own sword that sucked in even more light.

"You are greatly mistaken," answered Ometz. He held out his sword to Hash and whispered commandingly, "Take it!"

Hash's mind said, "What are you thinking?" but his heart said, "YES!" and he grasped the sword with both hands. Light blazed within his heart too as he charged the Being. When their swords met, the dark Being's sword shattered, and the being imploded into nothingness. Hash stood there holding the sword as a triumphal smile spread across his face.

Suddenly Grandfather also stood at his side. "That, my son, was courage." He held out his hand for the sword. Reluctantly Hash surrendered the weapon to him. Grandfather up-ended it, unscrewed its hilt, and dropped a stone into Hash's hand. "You wanted your stone? You now possess Ametz, the stone of Courage!"

"Grandfather," Hash responded sheepishly for one having just displayed so much courage, "can I have the sword too? I will put the stone back in its pommel."

Grandfather looked at Ometz, "And leave your angel without his sword?"

Hash dipped his head, "It was just a thought. Todah says, 'You have not because you ask not,' so I thought I should at least ask."

Grandfather smiled, "You will be fine with just the stone, and Todah is right. It never hurts to ask." Ometz was smiling too.

Chapter 10 -
In the World Not of It

I have sent you into the world. You need to be as wise and crafty as the Serpent himself, but behaving as harmlessly and innocently as a dove. Although for a time you were removed from the world, you are now ready to return to the world, having been transformed to wage warfare with divinely empowered weapons that will bring down the enemy's strongholds and demolish his lofty philosophy.

From the "Prophetic Readings of Scripture"

Their morning training had been another adventure in woodcraft. Hash was progressing very well with his stealth and never cheated by communicating with the animals. They had come back to the cave for lunch, and Hash had been left to do some practice on his talking to Chayeem and listening to His answers. Dal and Grandfather ventured back out into the forest.

Hash heard Chayeem say rather urgently, "You need to soak two of your blankets in the hot springs and fill two bowls with hot water, one large and one smaller." Hash had no sooner spread out the first of the soaked blankets on the ground when Grandfather walked in carrying an unconscious young man in his arms.

Grandfather smiled, "I see you have been talking to Chayeem." He placed the young man on the first of the warm blankets. "You can cover him with the second blanket, Hash. Besides having been beaten rather badly, I think he was beginning to suffer from exposure. He was very cold when I found him. Would you also fetch for me my healing herbs when you bring the larger bowl of hot water. Oh, and a face cloth. Thanks, Hash."

Hash quickly complied. He even brought an extra cloth for himself and assisted Grandfather by cleansing the visible wounds while Grandfather mixed the herbal ointment. Hash would then hand him a cloth, wash the dirty one clean, and trade him as he progressed through the wounds.

"Hash, could you make some tea in the smaller bowl, please." And he asked smiling. "Oh, and have I ever told you that I am very fond of you?"

"Yes, Grandfather," he was smiling in return, "often."

The young man remained unconscious, but from all appearances seemed to improve. He showed no fever or other signs of infection from his wounds. In fact, he seemed to sleep very deeply. Dal had arrived while they were finishing their tea, hopped up to his normal perch and began to debrief his aerial observation of the area where they had discovered the young man.

"It appears the young man was running from a small Triparteum attack team," began Dal. "I tracked them back to where they had entered the forest from the highway. Considering how far he made it into the woods before they caught him, he must be in incredible physical condition as it was one of the enemy's elite teams that was chasing him. He must not be infected with the Quicksilver tracker as they appeared to have had some difficulty finding him."

Quicksilver was the bioelectronic chip that the Triparteum required everyone to have implanted in the back of their wrist. Without it you could neither buy nor sell nor do business of any kind. It also contained a GPS function so the Triparteum's law enforcement always knew where you were, within inches. To not have a chip made this individual of special interest to Dal, Grandfather, and Hash.

"He must be one of the few remaining dissidents to not have a tracker," added Hash. "Do you suppose that was why they were chasing him and tried to kill him?"

"I do not think killing him was their objective," said Dal. "That would have been much easier to accomplish. They could have done that from a distance with their projectile weapons. No, this seemed personal. He appeared to have been beaten by hand."

"I guess we will have lots of questions for him when he awakens," added Grandfather. "Hash, you will need to keep an eye on him until he wakes up. He will undoubtedly be very confused and disoriented when he does."

"Okay, Grandfather," replied Hash.

While Hash watched over the sleeping young man, Grandfather cooked their meager evening meal. They lived rather spartanly in the cave, but it was a good life for which they were all grateful for the time being. What lay ahead, Chayeem had told them, would be much more difficult. After supper, they continued taking turns watching over the young man. During Dal's turn, Grandfather put Hash through his evening's mental, physical, and spiritual calisthenics ending with a long conversation with Chayeem, who shared with them that the lad's name was Abdul, which in Arabic means "the worshipper." He had been brought up as a follower of Islam, but that would soon change. They said good night to Chayeem, covered the stone, which lit the cavern with a basket so that it only let a little light out, and Dal and Grandfather went to bed. Hash had chosen the first shift of watching over Abdul while he slept.

Chapter 11 - I Dreamed

Their young men will see visions and their old men dream dreams (or sometimes the other way around).

From "Pastor Jon's Comments"

Early the next morning Abdul awoke and sat up with a start. He would have scrambled to his feet if it had not been for Grandfather's voice. "It's okay, Abdul. You are safe here."

He quickly looked around and began to relax. The combination of the environment of the cave and Grandfather's voice exuded safety and sanctity.

Then he exclaimed, "How do you know my name?"

Grandfather added, "We know some things about you, but there is much we don't know. It seems you were attacked by one of the Triparteum's elite forces teams. Perhaps, you could tell us why." He handed him a bowl of their morning mash. "You can eat that first, if you'd like."

"Thank you," said Abdul and proceeded to wolf down the mash. He handed Grandfather back the bowl. "Thank you for that and everything else it seems you have done for me." He looked at his clean and bandaged wounds.

"Would you like some more to eat?" Grandfather looked at the bowl as he continued. "Oh, let me introduce ourselves to you. I am simply called Grandfather by most people. This is Hash, and the hawk's name is Dal."

"No, that's fine for now," Abdul replied regarding the food. "Thank you again, and I am glad to meet all three of you," replied Abdul. "Let's see, where to start? The last thing I remember is being caught, thrown to the ground, beaten, and cursed. The Triparteum believe their chancellor to be a god, so they cursed me in his name. I thought they would kill me, but then I blacked out and that is all I remember, except the dream."

"You had a dream," asked Hash, "while you were recovering here?"

"Yes," Abdul replied with a far away look in his eye. "It was about a tree, a wondrous white tree. It stood two or three times the height of a man and had the most incredible iridescent fruit hanging from its branches. Oh, and it spoke to me."

"Really," said Hash smiling at Grandfather, "a talking Tree! And what did He say?"

"He? How do you know the tree is a he?" Abdul was puzzled, "Anyway, it said, 'Abdul, welcome. I have waited a long time to meet you.' How would this talking tree know my name? The dream seemed so real and I felt so at home there, like everything I had always been searching for I had suddenly found."

Dal finally spoke, "Because it was more than a dream. We know that Tree. We too have met Him. His name is Chayeem."

Abdul sat dumbfounded. A talking bird too? Dal had been sent on this mission with Hash and Grandfather partially because he could speak to and be understood by humans outside of the Sanctuary. Chayeem knew that would come in handy, as it did now.

Abdul finally found his voice, "The hawk can talk?" They all nodded. "And the tree?"

"The Tree actually exists and is a He," smiled Grandfather. "It is He that has sent us here, and it is He that sent you to us, in a round about sort of way. You see the Tree is a personification of God Himself."

"The tree is Allah?" Abdul sounded bewildered.

"No, He is greater than that," Grandfather tried desperately to be sensitive to Abdul's former faith. "He is the one you have always been searching for, even when you were following the ways of Allah."

"How can that be? There is only one God and Allah is his name!" which Abdul had firmly believed until only moments ago.

Dal took over at that point, "I think if you look deep within your heart you will find there is One greater; One who desperately loves you, and wants to have a relationship with you."

Still bewildered Abdul asked, "I can have a relationship with a tree?"

"With the God that the tree personifies, yes. You were designed to have a relationship with God, to be connected to Him, but you broke that connection with your wrong and the wrong now stands between you and your relationship to God. The wrong needs to be removed in order for you to be reconnected to God. You cannot remove your own wrong. You put it there. Someone else must remove your wrong for you. As a Muslim you believe that Jesus was a prophet and that He died?"

"Yes," Abdul responded tentatively, "we do."

"But why did He die?" asked Hash. "You also believe the four gospels, have you read them?

Abdul looked at his feet. "I started to once, but the first one started with a long genealogy and I gave up."

"Well, if you would have continued, you would have found out that He is much more than a prophet. Initially that's what people believed about Him, that He must be a prophet, but then He did things no other prophet ever did. Sure, Moses parted the Red Sea and Elisha raised a boy from the dead, but Jesus did this again, and again, and again. Sometimes He healed entire villages, besides casting out evil spirits and raising the dead. He also forgave people their sins. I don't recall a prophet ever doing that. Only God can forgive sins. And then He claimed that he was God, God's son, and when He died, He did so to take away my sin, your sin, the whole world's sin. And he didn't stay dead," Hash continued. "He came alive again and He would like to reconnect you to God. Would you like Him to do that for you, take away your wrong and reconnect you to God?"

Abdul looked around thinking. "Could this really be true? Could his wrong be removed? Could he actually have a relationship with God?" He wasn't even sure he knew what that meant, but his heart told him it was all he had ever wanted. Out loud he simply said, "Yes."

Hash then had Abdul ask Jesus to remove the wrong He had paid for with His death, and to reconnect him God. They then introduced him to Chayeem, who welcomed him. His dream was no longer just a dream; he felt he had come home.

They had a cup of tea and Abdul began to share with them current events in the world at large. He, his family, and their extended family had purchased a self-sustaining farm outside of the city in the nearby countryside. The buildings had been destroyed by fire and the owners, it seemed, died in the same fire. Their family had found the farm up for auction before the Quicksilver chip had been made mandatory for all financial transactions. The farm had its own well, plots that could be planted, and a few remaining farm animals. They bought the whole thing and began restoring the buildings. As soon as they deemed it was habitable they had moved in. They hoped it would become a retreat center for the expansion of Islam. However, the government began to put pressure on any religious organization that did not register with the state church and, eventually with any organization that did not proclaim the Triparteum chancellor Adonis, as god. The politics and economy began to polarize things, and people who tried to live outside of the state's control soon became destitute and homeless. Abdul's family's farm quickly became a refugee center for society's castaways, and that caused even more problems with the government. The Triparteum had increased taxes until finally it instituted an all-out persecution of any religion not part of the Tri-World Church. He and his family had been warned of an eminent military attack on their home and had fled the farm with only the clothes on their back. That is how he ended up being chased into the forest, caught, beaten, and left to die.

Abdul continued to describe the situation. "Although the Triparteum tries desperately to cover it up, poverty is rampant, as is sickness and despair. Homelessness is also at near epidemic proportions and it seems that the military and law enforcement arms of the government are more concerned with eliminating the people than with solving their problems. While I had thought I had found an answer to these things in the family of Islam, I now know that I was simply searching in the wrong place. Hope and satisfaction are only found in Jesus, the true Liberator, and in His Tree, Chayeem. Thank you for introducing me to Him."

They quickly nursed Abdul back to physical, emotional, and mental health. Only his spiritual health needed specific and practical training in cultivating his new relationship with the Tree. While more than a dozen years Hash's senior, he was humble enough to respect Hash's advanced relationship to Chayeem and learn from both him and Grandfather. While he initially considered Dal to be Grandfather's pet hawk, he soon found that all three of them considered each other as equals and depended on one another's unique gifts and talents. Then one evening after supper, Grandfather shared a most significant truth.

"Abdul," Grandfather began, "do you remember your dream you had when you were first recovering and how Chayeem shared that He had waited a long time to meet you?" Abdul nodded and Grandfather continued, "You and Hash have a very special place in His plans for the near future."

"We do?" Abdul replied, a bit astonished. He had never thought of himself as particularly special.

"Yes, it was foretold of old that in these Last Days, God would raise up two witnesses to confront the darkness and call the world back to Himself before the days of great judgment. You and Hash are those two witnesses."

"What?" Now it was Hash's turn to be astonished. "Abdul is going to join me as the other witness? Why haven't you told me about this before?"

"Because we haven't had time," smiled Grandfather. "Now we do."

"And how are we supposed to do this?" questioned Hash, Abdul adding his questioning gestures, "Confront the darkness?"

"Chayeem will lead you, just as He always has," said Grandfather, "and you will be protected from attack of the Enemy for a time."

"For a time, we will be protected for a time?" Hash did not think that sounded comforting. "And what does that mean?"

"Hash, you know the enemy can only destroy your body." Grandfather scolded him a bit. "No one can destroy you, either of you. You both now belong to Chayeem. Besides, after three days even your bodies will be revived and reunited with you to confound the enemy further."

Hash broke in, "I'm not particularly worried about being separated from my body…it's the getting there that bothers me. Shooting me with a projectile weapon is not a big deal, but torturing me to death slowly? Now that is another thing altogether. I don't relish that at all."

Abdul jumped in, giving Hash his own little smile, "Gee, if it's good enough for Grandfather and the Tree, it's good enough for me. We'll be okay, Hash."

Hash took a deep breath. Abdul had come a long way in just a short while. He gave a little sigh, "Yes, you both are right. Well, actually all of you are right. Forgive me my momentary lapse of faith. You just caught me a bit off guard. If you all say we will be okay then, I guess, we will. Let's go do this!"

PART 5 - FURTHER PREPARATION

Chapter 12 - If You Feed Them They Will Come

*I was **hungry and you fed me food,** I was thirsty and you gave me a drink, I was a stranger and you welcomed me in to your family, I was without clothes and you provided them for me, I was sick and you visited me, I was in prison and you came to me.*

Matthew 25:35-36

Eleazar met Judy and Julius at the cooking facility designated as Aleph, after the first letter in the Hebrew alphabet, for planning. They began by sharing what they envisioned would be the requirements needed to put together the food they would take along with each exploit team.

Eleazar began, "I was somewhat surprised to be asked to be one of the six that Chayeem called out as leaders. I don't particularly see myself as a leader."

Judy responded to him, "That might be one of the chief qualifications He was looking for, a basic dependence on Him coupled with an strong sense of humility."

"Hmm," echoed Eleazar, "I'd never thought of it quite like that, but I am rather humble," he chuckled as he said it.

"He does often have very different ideas than we do," added Julius. "I never really saw myself as a cook until my wife asked me to join her in helping feed the people here."

"So, how do you see this happening?" asked Eleazar.

"Well, in talking to Jon and looking at our current food production," said Julius, "it seems that God has already been getting things ready. Jon said this year's harvest of practically everything looks like it will be double what we normally need in the Sanctuary. However, that means we will require additional help harvesting it and bringing it to the food processing stations."

Eleazar continued, "That also says we will need double the folks to actually prepare and process the food. Oh, and then there are the additional requirements to package it somehow for delivery on each exploit."

Judy added, "I think we have our work cut out for us. Should we ask Chayeem whom He wants to orchestrate what?" Both

Julius and Eleazar nodded, so she prayed, "Chayeem, it seems that you have three of us here and there are new requirements to provide food for the exploit teams to take along to feed the hungry: additional harvesters, processors, and packagers. Oh, and a need for transportation is in there somewhere, too. Who would you like to lead each of those endeavors?"

Eleazar spoke first, "I believe He would have me help Jon with the harvest and I would love to do that."

"He wants me to be a part of the food processing," added Judy.

"I guess that leaves me with packaging, but I was leaning that way anyway," said Julius. "Now we just have to see who shows up after lunch and which team they feel they are supposed to join." Judy and Eleazar smiled and nodded their assent.

About one hundred and fifty folk showed up after lunch to become a part of the "feed the hungry" teams. Eleazar explained what he, Judy, and Julius had planned and prayed through with Chayeem. He then asked for a show of hands, hoofs, paws, and wings, of those who had experience in the areas of harvesting and food processing. About two-thirds of them raised their hands, wings, or paws. He asked if their heart desired to continue working in these areas and most of the heads nodded. He had them join Judy and himself and gave the floor to Julius.

Julius asked if any of the remaining folks, who had no prior experience with harvesting or food processing desired to join those teams and gain some experience. About another twenty people raised their hands, and he dismissed them to join those respective teams.

"So, I guess that means the rest of you want to join me on the packaging teams?" he asked. A general head nodding ensued and he led them, about thirty of them, over to some of the dining room tables.

"Just because I have been appointed leader doesn't mean I know what to do, have all the answers, or will make all the decisions," said Julius. "I would love to have us figure this out together, as a team. So, what are your ideas on how we, the agrarian society that we are, can package food for delivery to the poor and homeless back in the city?"

Caleb raised a paw, "There are a number of large leaves we could use to wrap around the food and we make our own twine. We could use that to tie them up."

"Great idea, Caleb," Julius responded. "What else?"

They continued to brainstorm ideas and work through them until they all felt they had developed a workable plan. It did, however, take most of the remaining afternoon to flesh out the details.

Chapter 13 - Surprise

We do not see what we are not looking for, except when we have assistance.

From the "Musings of the Wise Man"

It was a beautiful summer morning, but then every day in the Sanctuary seemed like that. Bigtha was walking in her garden when she discovered a number of her vegetables had wilted. Normally everything flourished in the Sanctuary. Upon further examination of the plants in question, she discovered that someone or something had eaten their roots. Since she had been given the responsibility of tending and caring for the garden, she considered it a personal affront on her calling and destiny. She was incensed or closer to down right angry. It seemed that evil had entered the Sanctuary. This kind of behavior could not be tolerated. It needed to be rooted out. She tried a number of ways to trap the culprit, but all to no avail. Finally, completely exasperated, she went to the Tree. She probably should have gone to Him sooner.

She bowed before the Tree, "Pardon me, Chayeem, but somehow, since the attack on the entrance to your Sanctuary, an evil has entered here. Something is eating the roots of some of my vegetables and killing them. This has never happened before. I have been unable to trap the culprit and deal with it, so I come to you for help."

Chayeem chuckled under His breath, "Does it not seem strange to you, Bigtha, that I should be your last resort rather than your first?"

Bigtha hung her head lower, "I thought that I could take care of it myself and not concern You with it."

Chayeem's voice still seemed smiling, "You know of course, Bigtha, that you do not need to be standing in front of me in order to talk to me."

Although a grown woman, she suddenly felt like a little child, although not diminished or devalued in any way. "Yes sir, I am sorry. I should have asked you sooner," she said haltingly.

"That's okay, Bigtha, we can take care of this now, but we could have avoided your consternation had you come to me earlier," the Tree continued. "So who do you think is responsible for this," He chuckled again, "problem?"

"Some rodent I would assume," said Bigtha.

"An evil rodent?" questioned Chayeem. "Are there any evil beings in my Sanctuary?"

"That is why I was concerned, Sir," she tried to explain herself. "This seemed so uncharacteristic."

"Ah, yes," the Tree went on, "new things are often difficult. They don't fit the pattern of the past and their differentness seems to make them wrong, evil as you would say."

Bigtha began to smile herself. "I think I am supposed to prepare myself for a lesson?"

'Perhaps" continued the Tree. "Bigtha, I would like to introduce you to a friend of mine." Out of the ground popped the head of a gopher. "This is Diggory, he is new to our congregation. I believe he is," He emphasized the words, "*your culprit.*" The Tree shook one of His limbs and one of His fruit fell to the ground between the three of them. "Could you give him a bite? Then I think you can have a little chat."

Bigtha knelt, took out her knife, cut a slice of Chayeem's fruit and offered it to Diggory. He took it in his paws, nibbled on it for a minute, and then looked directly into Bigtha's eyes.

"Chayeem told me that we could become friends. Is that possible?" asked Diggory. "Oh, and I am sorry for eating from your garden without asking." He reached out a paw, like he was about to shake her hand.

Bigtha reached out a finger and touched the paw. "I accept your apology and yes, I think we may become friends." She paused, "In fact, I would be honored to be your friend, if you will have me."

Diggory nodded, they both turned to the Tree, bowed, thanked Him, and left the garden together.

Chapter 14 -
And We Need to
Clothe Them Too

*I was hungry and you fed me food, I was thirsty and you gave me a drink, I was a stranger and you welcomed me into your family, **I was without clothes and you provided them for me**, I was sick and you visited me, I was in prison and you came to me.*

Matthew 25:35-36

Kate, Logan, and Tanaheil met to discuss, strategize, and plan for the "clothe the naked" portion of their future exploits. The last few people to find safety inside the Sanctuary had brought with them tales of the increasing failure of the Triparteum economy, which created an epidemic of poverty and homelessness. So, partnered with "feed the hungry" they planned to position themselves to make a significant difference with the new exploits and with all of the gifts functioning in harmony. As they adventured back into the city's streets, they would not only draw numbers of people out to be ministered to but they would creatively win the right to be heard.

Because the Sanctuary grew its own cotton, raised its own silk worms, and had plenty of sheep born these last few years, they had plenty of raw materials from which to manufacturer everything. They only needed the raw manpower (using the term loosely) to make it happen and, due to the recent outpouring of giftedness, even that no longer posed a problem. With Kate and Logan partnering to orchestrate the animal division and Tanaheil leading the human and angelic divisions, they began to set in place the processes needed to supply finished articles of bedding, blankets, clothing and sandals.

While the transition from planning to production was by no means seamless, the strength of their combined vision, the work of Chayeem's Spirit, and the general cooperation of everyone soon had everything up and running. The entire clothing division often found themselves humming and singing during their labors and it turned the repetitiveness of production into an act of worship. The singing facilitated it, but so did everything about "how" they accomplished their tasks. Also interestingly, each week at their worship and celebration together before the Tree and the Pillar of Fire, Meezimore, Todah, Piper, and José would debut a new worship song and that song would capture their hearts and minds all week long. Soon they found their stockpiles of completed goods ready for final assembly into transportable bundles.

Within only a few short weeks they had progressed from gathering raw materials to the stage of finally being able to deliver family and individual bundles of their finished goods. That Sabbath, as they rested from their week's labor, the clothing division held a time of celebration right after their general celebration before the Tree and the Pillar of Fire. They all gathered around the pile of bundles that they had produced that week to offer praise and thanksgiving for what they could now provide to the exploit teams. A number of individuals stood up one by one and expressed specific thankfulness to the effort that a particular individual or group had put into reaching this milestone. One or more individuals thanked every step of the process as an entire atmosphere of gratefulness seemed to permeate the group. Finally, Kate, Logan, and Tanaheil stood up to a thunderous round of applause that ended in a standing ovation. Unnoticed by them all, Meezimore crept in and suddenly led out in another new and incredible song of worship and praise. He was joined by the entire angel contingency that was there. Soon everyone joined in to create a cacophony of joy. They now stood ready to fully support the exploit teams as they gathered to re-enter the Triparteum's failing society.

Chapter 15 -
We Need to Set Them
Free

*The Spirit of the Lord is upon me, because he has
anointed me to proclaim good news to the poor.
He has sent me to proclaim liberty to the captives
and recovering of sight to the blind,
to set at liberty those who are oppressed,
to proclaim the year of the Lord's favor."*

Luke 4:18-19

Aaron and Alathos stood before the Tree. Azinath, the great eagle, stood on Alathos' back as they listened to the Tree. "I must admit that sometimes I find you all quite interesting. I know that may be difficult for you to understand, since I know everything, but still...," He paused for dramatic effect, "it's true. You have very little problem with the hospitality gifts or even with worship and proclamation, but when it comes to signs and wonders, that's another story."

Somewhat reluctant to interrupt Chayeem, Aaron interjected, "I think it may have something to do with the requirement to be completely dependent on You and an intimacy with you for which few are willing to pay the price."

"And yet," continued the Tree, "why is dependency on Me so hard? I designed you to be connected to Me, to walk in fellowship with Me. What is it about a relationship with Me that you fear? Why can't we just be friends?" He seemed a bit exasperated.

Aaron added, "As You know each of us turned away from You at an early age and walked apart from You for much of our life. We became habitually independent. We are all like Meshar, who was trained as a warrior from his birth. In order to become a warrior for You he had to relearn to fight in an entirely different way. Each of us must relearn to live in interdependency with You."

"Well, Aaron, my friend," admitted the Tree, "you have come a long way in that regard since the day we first met."

"Thank You, Sir," Aaron bowed, "but how can we take years of learning to become dependent on You and quickly pass that on to others in preparation for these next series of exploits?"

"Ah," intoned the Tree deeply, "the root of discipleship is to show them how to do it, and then let them do it. Alathos will show you the portal that leads to the city center. You will go and conveniently and graciously, I might add, kidnap a likely candidate, whom I will show you, and bring them back here to be the first subject for our discipling demonstrations. It will probably be easiest for us to start with a blind person. Is that okay with you, Alathos?"

"Certainly, my Lord." Alathos bowed.

"Azinath, you will provide aerial support, covering, and protection," said the Tree.

Azinath rustled his feathers proudly, "Yes, Sir."

And Alathos?" sang the Tree.

"I know," smiled Alathos. "You're very fond of me."

"You said it! In fact I am very fond of all three of you," chuckled the Tree.

The three of them stopped by Aaron's to grab his day pack and by the cooking facilities for a light lunch to take with them, just in case, and some water. Then Alathos led them to an unobtrusive meadow and said, "Simply cross the meadow and don't forget from where you emerge."

Azinath said, "Okay," and launched himself off Alathos' back. He flew halfway across the meadow and disappeared from view, with a puff.

"It's as simple as that," Alathos winked at Aaron, who smiled a bit sheepishly and began to walk across the meadow. Halfway across the meadow he suddenly emerged into a darkened alley between two tall, dilapidated city buildings. Azinath stood atop of a nearby garbage bin.

"I'll bet you're glad I went first," laughed Azinath. "I nearly fell out of the sky with shock when I suddenly found myself flying down this alley. Would you like to turn around and walk back twenty paces to make sure we can return to the meadow?"

Aaron swallowed and reluctantly turned around, walking back the way he had come. Without warning he found himself in the meadow again. Alathos stood there with a big grin on his face.

Aaron asked, "How come no one finds that alley and crosses over into the Sanctuary?"

Alathos continued smiling, "You said it, they have to *find* the alley." Aaron turned around and went back into the alley with garbage everywhere. Azinath was still perched on his garbage bin.

"Do you suppose they don't know there is a bin there?" asked Aaron pointing to the bin where Azinath stood. "It would seem pretty easy to clean up this alley and put all the garbage in the bin."

"With all the apathy and depression caused by this environment, I imagine the general response to your question would be, 'Why, who cares,'" responded Azinath. The smile had left his voice. "Do you want me to do a little aerial surveillance first, or shall we just head off in that direction?" He pointed down the alley with his beak.

Aaron cocked his head a little to one side, which he often did when listening to Chayeem, and said, "Surveillance."

He returned almost immediately, "There is a street just beyond those boxes that mark the end of the alley. Take a left and on the next corner is a blind beggar."

Aaron walked down the alley past the boxes and onto the sidewalk. Just as Azinath had said, on the street corner to the left sat a blind man begging. Aaron approached him. Not a prosperous part of town, but not the slums either, the street looked fairly deserted for the moment. The man seemed in his fifties and the state of his shabby clothing attested to his long association with his current situation. The man held a sign, "I am blind, a little food would help a lot. Bless you." His red and white "I am blind" walking stick lay propped up against the building next to him.

"Good morning, friend," began Aaron as he crouched next to him. "My name is Aaron. What's yours?"

"Nathaniel, but my friends call me Nate," he smiled. He still had most of his teeth. "You don't happen to have any food with you that you could spare?"

"No, Nate, I don't, but I could take you where there is some," Aaron added.

Nate's smile lessened, "Why should I trust you?"

"Here," Aaron continued, "take my hand." Aaron waited to see if he would reach out his hand and Nate did. Aaron grasped his hand and held it for a moment. The beginning of a kind of friendship bond passed between them.

Nate's smile returned, "Okay!" Aaron grasped his arm and helped him up. Aaron took the sign, handed Nate his walking stick, and wrapped Nate's other hand through his own arm at the elbow.

"How well do you know this area?" Aaron asked.

"Pretty well, I come here almost every day. You could say this is my corner," Nate added with assurance.

"We are going to go half way up the block and turn right down the alley between the buildings. There are no obstacles along the way," Aaron said.

Nate pulled on his arms, "You can't go down that alley, it's blocked off."

"Not today it isn't." Aaron was on Nate's street side and began to walk down the sidewalk, taking Nate with him. Nate tapped his cane on the sidewalk three times, then swung it to the right and the left about a foot and then started tapping again as they went. When they got to the alley, Aaron turned and stopped. "You can check with your cane and see that the alley is open today." Nate did. As they stepped forward down the alley Aaron spoke calmly, "I'd like to introduce you to my friend Azinath. You can trust him too."

"Azinath, that's an interesting name. Well, if he's your friend..." Nate seemed only a little concerned.

Azinath added reassuringly, "It's ancient Hebrew. Some say it means eagle."

Nate's concern lifted, "Well, you don't sound like an eagle."

Azinath laughed, "I don't know, what do eagles sound like? Maybe I look like one, sharp nose, beady eyes," he was clearly enjoying this as he hopped ahead of them.

Nate stopped cold the moment they entered the meadow and his cane no longer clicked on the alley pavement. "Wait a minute, where are we? What is that smell? It smells like pine trees."

"It is pine trees, Nate," said Aaron. "Welcome home. We call this place the Sanctuary and we have come here to give you back your sight. I just need to take you to some of my other friends. It that okay?"

Tears slowly flowed down Nate's cheeks. He stopped, took his hand from Aaron's arm, got out a handkerchief, and dried his eyes, "There are rumors that a place like this exists, but I thought it was all make-believe."

Aaron startled, "Really, rumors of the Sanctuary exist out there in your world? What do they say?"

"The rumors are many and varied," continued Nate, "but in all of them there is a consistent thread. Some people say that they have even seen it in their dreams. They say that God has not left us, but has prepared a place for us. It is not a place of escape, but a place of preparation, to make us ready to live forever, a place that frees us from ourselves and equips us to make a difference, but I didn't really believe it existed."

"Yep, it's real and we are here," said Azinath as he flew off ahead of them. When they had entered the Sanctuary another man was standing in Alathos the centaur's usual spot.

As the man stepped silently towards them, Aaron shared, "And here is Justice to assist us along the way. If you give him your cane, he will take your other hand under his arm and we can walk a little faster. Again, there are no obstacles along the way we will be going." Nate held out the cane, Justice took it, and then took Nate's hand and placed it around his arm. Together the three of them walked arm in arm back to their meeting area.

By the time they arrived, Azinath had gathered the signs and wonders team. Aaron sat Nate down in their midst and tried to explain what would happen next.

"Nate, there are about two dozen people here. Well, actually some of them are human, some are angels, and some are animals. I don't want you to be too surprised when you can finally see them. They are all learning how to heal people. I will show them how with you and then we will go back to the city and get a couple more people, bring them back here, and then give each of my friends a turn at healing them. Are you still okay with all of this?"

Nate nodded, "Yup!"

"My friends," Aaron addressed the group, "healing is simple, much simpler than you realize. It is simply asking Chayeem what He would like us to do and then doing it."

Nate raised his hand, "Who's Chayeem?"

Azinath responded, "He is the physical representation of God in our midst. He's a Tree."

"You worship a tree?" Nate said astonished.

"Not exactly," continued Azinath, "but bear with us for a few minutes and then I will take you to meet Him."

Aaron spoke out loud, "Chayeem, how would you like me to proceed? I didn't have to say that out loud, but I did so that those of you around me could hear." He cocked his head to the side, as was his habit and then asked, "Nate, I'd like you to stand, turn around, and kneel in front of the chair in which you are sitting. Then I am going to sit in that chair." Nate did what was asked of him and Aaron sat in the chair, took Nate's head in his two hands, and breathed on him. Nate closed his eyes when Aaron's hands touched his head. When he opened them back up, he could see.

"What?!" Nate exclaimed. He looked up at Aaron, turned his head left and right, and then turned around and sat on the ground. He continued to exclaim, "I can see all of you, I can see!"

Everyone who could kneel instantly fell to their knees and a cacophony of praise rose from their multitude of voices. Aaron let it go on for a few minutes and then stood and raised his hand for silence. "It's that easy. I simply asked Chayeem what he wanted me to do, did it, and Nate is healed of his blindness."

Nate was still sitting flabbergasted. He had been blind so long. Aaron addressed the eagle, "Azinath, if you would like to take Nate to meet Chayeem, I will take Justice back with me and we will return with a couple other people," he pointed to the crowd, "for you to heal in the way Chayeem shows you."

Azinath responded, "It would be my privilege to take Nate to meet Chayeem."

Craning his neck around, Nate almost fell over, "You really are an eagle, and you talk!"

"Yes, I am," responded Azinath, "and, yes, I do. You will find that we all talk and understand one another here. It's part of the wonder of this place. Now, if you will just follow me."

Nate got hesitantly to his feet and followed the eagle who flew in the direction of the Tree. Azinath looked over his shoulder and said, "Oh, there will be a Pillar of Fire there with the Tree, but it's okay. They are together."

Aaron and Justice walked off towards the meadow while the rest of the congregation milled around and shared the wonderfulness of what they had all just experienced. They came back with two more blind people, and others healed them. Then they brought back some crippled children, and they were healed. Over the next few weeks they brought back others, even some mentally ill people, and they, too, were set free and restored to their right mind. After each wonder, someone had the privilege to take that person to meet Chayeem and that felt like the frosting on the cake. Each person on the team had a chance to participate in someone's healing or deliverance, and their confidence and dependency on Chayeem reached an all-time high because of each unique situation, circumstance, and person. Then Chayeem called a general assembly for the following morning.

PART 6 - ENEMY BACKLASH

Chapter 16 - Triparteum Response

Evil will get worse and worse until it seems to fully engulf the good, until every thought and intention of the heart of man is wicked and perverse continually. The desires of the Dragon will have become the wishes of the people, and it will seem that there no longer is any hope of righteousness or justice.

From the "Return to an Antediluvian Age"

Kouta announced, entered into the Chancellor's private chamber. Adonis sat at a large, ornately, carved ivory desk reading and signing papers. There was an administrative assistant at his left hand with a stack of papers that she summarized for him before she handed them to him for his signature. He still quickly scanned each one of them before he signed them, because once signed, they were law. To his right stood a large armchair with an ornate ivory base carved to match the desk. In that chair, designed for him, sat Adonis' son, the humanoid Ben, in some kind of meditative trance.

Ben snapped out of the trance and addressed the assistant, "Please, excuse yourself Miss, and what was your name again?"

She blanched noticeably, "My name is of no consequence, my Lord," bowed and quickly exited.

Ben shook his head at the woman and then focused his attention on his general, "Yes, Kouta, what do you have to report?"

Kouta had taken a knee between them, unsure whom to address. "My Lords, we have identified over a dozen enclaves of dissidents in the surrounding countryside, within a one hundred mile radius of the city limit. They consist of individuals who have banded together to subvert our economy. They are mostly farms and farmers that raise food and barter it with one another."

Adonis had lifted his eyes and scowled deeply at the word dissidents. "What economic sanctions can we bring about on these rebels?"

Kouta scowled too. "The resources expended to discover this were minimal. We initially picked up and correlated their movements from the analysis of our security drone activity, but to take any action against them would probably be cost prohibitive. We have yet to discover any general market gathering of them."

Ben volunteered, "I could fly out there and do some investigating."

Adonis responded, now smiling, "Your presence would be a bit conspicuous."

Ben stated flatly, "Which might prove to be an adequate deterrent to their further rebellious dealings with one another."

"Hmmm, I will think about that," Adonis mused. "In the meantime, Kouta, see if any of your men can infiltrate their organization, perhaps hiring on as a seasonal farm hand. We will let that suffice for the time being."

Kouta got up off his knee, bowed to each of them, and left the chambers. Ben turned his gaze to the landscape framed by the large projectile-proof picture window behind Adonis' desk. "The Luminescent One is disturbed by the continued guerrilla assaults of the Virgin's children. Either we did not destroy their headquarters or enough of them escaped the destruction to build another one somewhere else. There is also the problem of her two witnesses who frequent the city square almost daily. They appear to be indestructible."

Adonis' smile had turned upside down again. "Yes, they are a nuisance, although they are not getting nearly the response that they did initially. Nevertheless, he continues to assure me that we are close to discovering a means to defeat those two demons. Perhaps you should pay them another visit. Has your meditation provided you access to any other weapons? Perhaps you and Baalel need to make another visit to my sacred meditation center and its black altar."

"My meditations have only firmed my resolve to defeat them," which was obvious by the set of his jaw, "but they have not provided me with any additional weapons. A visit to the black altar is a great idea. Do you know where Baalel is?"

"Search your heart," snapped Adonis. "I am sure he lurks somewhere near!"

"Ah!" Ben exclaimed, "Found him. Thank you Father." He got up out of the chair, bowed to his father, and left the room.

Adonis reached down and with right thumbprint unlocked the bottom drawer. He took out the ancient manuscript, flipped to the final pages, and began reading carefully. Eliminating the two witnesses would also lead to the discovery of the rebels' sanctuary, and that would lead to the final assault and victory. He could hardly wait.

Chapter 17 -
Economic Sanctions

How will we reach into the heart of our enemy and
rip it out? We must first pretend we are one of them.
We do, after all, follow the angel of light.

From the "Musings of the Beast"

L ieutenant Jacob Laban had been promoted to his current post when the special forces lost its most elite member, Gomed Akkub. Gomed, who had been sent on a special assignment, to locate the rebel's headquarters, had never been heard from again and was presumed captured and/or killed. Jacob had now become one of a few people who knew Kouta's secret place even existed. As a worshipper of the elemental forces, Kouta had constructed his own black altar, not knowing it replicated almost exactly the one in Adonis' own meditation center. Cuttings from Kouta's weekly ceremonies crisscrossed his arms. Fresh blood from his latest cut pooled on the altar and he lay prostrate before it. After only one visit to Kouta's sacred place, Jacob still struggled to repress his fear and excitement. He wasn't at all sure if he should disturb Kouta's supplications so he just stood waiting. Should he even be seeing this or should his eyes be closed and his head bowed? Maybe he should be kneeling in reverence or prostrate too. In Kouta's army he knew all the protocol, but here he felt out of his depth. As he was starting to kneel Kouta stirred and with agility amazing for a man his size leapt to his feet in a single fluid movement.

With a wicked smile of satisfaction on his face he turned to face Jacob, "Lieutenant Laban, good to see you. You are right-handed are you not?" Jacob nodded. "Let me see your right palm." As he extended his hand, palm upward, Kouta drew his knife and sliced it so quickly that it seemed the cut had just materialized out of thin air and appeared on his palm. "Please make a fist and squeeze some blood onto the altar to join mine." When he did there was a flash of light, and behind the altar stood an angel of indescribable light and beauty. Again at a loss as to what to do, he simply followed Kouta's lead and took one knee. "My Lord, I have brought Lieutenant Laban as you requested." Jacob kept his head bowed, but found it difficult not to gaze on such beauty. He had to be satisfied to only look at the angel's feet. The boots the angel wore sparkled up his calf as though they contained innumerable jewels. Jacob could not separate illusion from reality. Then the angel spoke, and breath left Jacob's lungs.

The air vibrated as if all the music of the cosmos played an accompaniment to the angel's words. "I have waited a long time for this moment, Jacob. I have an assignment for you that I don't believe any other human being on the planet could accomplish." The pride that filled Jacob's chest brought tears to his eyes though he never, ever cried. The angel continued, "There are a number of farms outside the city that are living in open rebellion to the chancellor's government. I want you to infiltrate one of them. Hire on as a farmhand or some other kind of laborer and discover for me and Kouta," he added somewhat condescendingly, "just how we may destroy them. An open attack would be too conspicuous and too easy. Besides, I want to wound them at their very core, not just obliterate them!" The ground vibrated with the venomous power behind those words and the music behind them had completely altered. Like a candle snuffed out, he vanished, leaving a decidedly dark space around the altar.

Kouta sneered, "Can you do this for our Lord?"

Jacob wondered silently if Kouta questioned why he had not been given the task himself, but then Jacob was not nearly seven feet tall with the physique of a god. He smiled at himself and his undistinguished features and perhaps he gloated a bit unconsciously. He replied, "Yes, sir, I most certainly can."

"Good," Kouta spat out, "our final offensive depends on it."

"Am I dismissed then, sir?" Jacob said almost a little too impertinently.

"Yes! And leave your transmitter on at all times." Kouta was still spitting.

"I'm sorry, sir, but it will be impossible for me to successfully infiltrate the rebels wearing a transmitter. I will simply check in as often as I can. You'll just have to trust me for that," he said. He hoped the smirk did not show on his face or in his voice.

"I guess that will have to do," snapped Kouta. "Dismissed!" Jacob left, still smiling to himself.

Chapter 18 - Infiltration

The best way to destroy an enemy is from the inside. Victory is the sweetest when you are able to betray someone who considered you a trusted friend.

From the "Strategies on War"

A lie is the most difficult to detect when it sticks very closely to the truth. The same is true of a disguise. Deception achieved with as little change as possible, has the greatest chance of escaping detection. Herein lay one of Jacob's greatest talents. Nothing about him drew attention, so when he desired to look a certain way, like a common laborer, he fairly easily did so. He simply donned the garments of a laborer and changed his speech. Thus attired he walked out of the city. He chose to walk the dirt country roads, picking up an additional layer of dust and dirt from passing vehicles to make his dirty clothes more travel worn. He made his way to one of the farms that Kouta had identified as being in the rebel network, and walked up to a man who had an air of authority.

"My name is Jacob. I've heard you can use some help before the harvest," Jacob ventured. "I need work."

"Juan Carlos," They shook hands. "Who have you worked for in these parts?"

"I'm new in this area, but…" He showed his hands, obviously used to hard work. The rest of his physique, while undistinguished, had the same toughened appearance.

"Well, I need some work on the machinery. Do you have any experience with that?" responded the farmer.

"Yes." He had to be careful, as he had almost added, "Sir." He continued, "Years ago in the army I trained in a tractor division, bulldozing roads."

"Hmmm," continued the farmer, "the pay is not great, mostly credits to our co-op store, we have an informal network of farms here, but the food is good, the bed warm, and the housing clean and dry. How about we try you for a few weeks and see."

"Seems fair," replied Jacob. "When can I start?" He had a battered old army duffle bag with him.

"Stow your stuff in the bunkhouse," said the farmer. "You'll find my son Joe in the barn. Tell him I'm trying you out."

Again, he felt tempted to salute, but he refrained. He stopped by the bunkhouse, left his duffle bag on one of the many empty beds, and reported to the barn.

In the barn he found a pair of coverall-clad legs on a creeper, jutting out from beneath a tractor. The boots looked old and warn, probably hand-me-downs. Jacob made more noise than usual as he approached. He didn't want to startle Joe.

He crouched down to be more at Joe's level and offered, "Joe, your dad just brought me on to help get ready for harvest, name's Jacob." He extended a hand of greeting under the tractor.

"I'd shake your hand, but mine's all greasy," offered Joe. "Could you pass me a 9/16" socket?"

The toolbox near Joe appeared very well organized. The socket tray out of the toolbox on the floor had all the sockets arranged by size, as well as the open-end and box-end wrenches. There was a 1/2" socket missing from the tray. Jacob removed the 9/16" socket from the tray and reached it under the tractor. Joe gave him the 1/2" in exchange. Before putting it put back in the tray, Jacob first grabbed a rag and wiped it clean.

Joe slid out from under the tractor, wiped his hands clean, sat up and said, "Now I can shake your hand." Jacob extended his again. "Pleased to meet you, Jacob." He looked down as he replaced 9/16" socket and noticed Jacob had wiped the 1/2" one clean. "How's your machinery experience?"

Jacob went to attention, complete with salute, "Five years Army, sir, tractor division." and smiled.

Joe smiled in return, "Wheel bearings?"

Jacob still stood at attention, "Plenty, sir." He broke his salute and laughed.

"Well, good, because we're repacking those next," said Joe still smiling. "I think we might become friends."

"I hope so," added Jacob and started to roll up his sleeves. As he did, Joe noticed his scar from the insertion of the Quicksilver chip.

Joe's smile faded, "You have the chip."

"Yes," replied Jacob, "everyone in the Army has them, in fact they are mandatory for everyone period."

Joe showed him both of his wrists, "We don't. I hope that won't be a problem."

"Not for me," said Jacob, "but how do you buy and sell without one?"

"One member of the Co-op has one, but we are mostly self-sustaining and don't need him to use it. We sort of live under the government's radar. I hope that's not a problem either."

"Not for me," he said a bit sadly. "The government and I are not on the best of terms. I got in a fight with an officer who gave me an order I couldn't in good conscience complete. I ended up getting discharged. I have been a bit homeless for a while now. That's why I need this job."

"Well, not a problem with me," said Joe. "Let's attack this wheel, shall we?"

A simple "Yup," was all he needed to say.

They had two of the wheels done by lunch and after they cleaned up as well as they could and went into house to eat, Joe took his dad aside and praised Jacob's work for both its quantity and quality.

Chapter 19 - Farmers' Weekend

The more information you gather on your enemy, the closer you are to victory. Identify their strengths and their weaknesses, as both can be used effectively against them.

From the "Strategies on War"

After a full week of working on the machinery, Juan Carlos, his wife Maria, Joe, and the rest of the family wondered how they had ever gotten along before Jacob had joined them. Not only did he work tirelessly, but he behaved like the consummate gentleman and servant around the house. Whatever needed to be done, he offered to help and pitched right in to make it happen.

He even nicely made suggestions on how to make life easier for Maria and their eldest daughter Beth alike, "Why don't we lay some pipe from the hand pump to a water cache in the kitchen?" He designed it one evening and he and Joe got up earlier than usual the next few mornings, found some discarded pipe in the barn, and had it installed by Friday. It also soon became obvious that Beth had a crush on Jacob, and then the gentleman side of him shone brightly. He never made a pass at her, but always treated both her and her mother as royalty. Each evening the entire family, including Jacob now, met in the living room after supper and Juan Carlos would tell them a story about the one they called the Liberator, Jesus. Jacob later found out from Joe that his father had virtually memorized these stories from his father. All the stories came from their sacred scriptures. No actual copies of these scriptures existed anymore, but one parent taught them to the children, and in each family one child always proved particularly adept at learning the stories. That child guaranteed that the stories would then be passed down to the following generation. It also became apparent that they believed these stories were true, and Jacob realized soon that he would have to come to terms with this Jesus person on more than just an intellectual level. They did not consider Jesus to be just an historical figure that had died thousands of years ago. They actually believed that He still lived, and they prayed to Him, sang to Him, worshipped Him. They considered Him God, like Jacob was supposed to consider the chancellor. Jacob had met the chancellor and, while he was powerful, extremely powerful, he did not strike Jacob as being a god.

That Saturday, the Josephsons hosted the Farmers Market's store. They moved the store around seemingly at random to make it more difficult for the government to keep tabs on them, one of the reasons Kouta had dispatched Jacob and assigned him to figure out what would hurt them most economically. However, Jacob was beginning to wonder if he would be able to complete this assignment or if he would end up discharged again, like in his story, which had been mostly true. He thought of a number of scenarios, but hesitated to share any of them with headquarters. He had grown much too fond of these really good people in only a week. They were all so kind to him. He liked and admired them all. They all worked very hard and cared deeply about each other and even, it seemed, to genuinely care about him. As he perused the market he continued to be impressed with everyone's friendliness and with how quickly they assimilated him into their group. If Juan Carlos vouched for you, that satisfied all of them.

After the market, he left to visit the city. He truthfully said that he had a few other things stored in a locker, but he also needed to touch bases with headquarters. He took his empty duffle bag with him. Joe offered to go along, but he declined the offer tactfully. Instead, he hitched a ride with one of the other market attendees for most of the way. A meeting with Kouta took priority. He scanned his wrist upon entry to the building, which meant that Kouta was instantly aware of his presence. He stopped off at the rest room to freshen up from the trip and to actually make Kouta wait a few minutes, a tactical ploy, but useful. It leveled the playing field a little.

Chapter 20 - Strategic Planning

The more options you can identify and carefully consider, the better your chances at finding the optimal strategic plan.

From the "Strategies on War"

Kouta waited behind his desk, his back towards the door as he looked out the large picture window with his hands carelessly clasped behind his back. It put him in an incredibly vulnerable position, but maybe it just meant that he did not consider Jacob a threat. That or he thought himself fast enough to counter anything anyone would possibly attempt in the confines of his large office.

"Lieutenant Laban, what do you report?" He did not even turn around.

"Sir," Jacob began, "I have successfully infiltrated the rebel farming organization." Since Kouts's back was turned, he could not read the slight smile on Jacob's face. Jacob held himself in check though, in case Kouta could see his reflection in the window.

"And what have you discovered, Lieutenant?" A hardness edged Kouta's words.

"I'm not sure they are really worth the effort, sir, but their weekly markets are moved from farm to farm on an apparently random basis. I have yet to discover the pattern," Jacob admitted.

Kouta turned in the blink of an eye and slammed his palm on the desk. "They are rebels, they need to become an example. The world must know that you cannot defy the chancellor or you will be punished!" Palatable anger thickened the air.

"If we truly want to make an example of them, it will take more time. Whatever the chancellor does must cripple their entire network not just effect a simple rebellious farm or two." Jacob opined.

Kouta stiffened to his full, imposing height, "Do you think to lecture me on strategy and tactics?"

Jacob lowered his head, "No, sir, just making an observation. That is why you sent me in, sir."

"Humph, maybe that was a mistake!" Kouta spat.

"I think, sir, that you will find our covert action much more successful and satisfying in fulfilling the chancellor's directive than any direct strike would have been. When we have completed this operation he will be extremely appreciative of the efficiency and effectiveness with which you carried out his orders."

"That remains to be seen, Lieutenant. How much more time?" He had calmed down a little.

"I should have a much better idea in another week," ventured Jacob.

"See that you do. Dismissed!" And he turned back to the window.

Jacob left feeling pretty good about the meeting. Sometimes using kid gloves with Kouta failed, but this time they seemed sufficient. He traveled to his storage locker and picked up the books and other items he wanted to take back to the farm, his excuse for coming into the city in the first place. He loaded them in his duffle, and walked out towards the highway. Like his predecessor, Gomed, Jacob's success as an incredible soldier and warrior came because he fought for all the right reasons. His belief in truth, justice, that might should support right, that it was the government's responsibility to serve and protect; all of these supported his actions and helped him to live in a state of physical, mental, and spiritual balance.

On his way back to the countryside, he skirted the city square. Intrigued by the sound of a large commotion he decided to take a look. Surely a peek would cause no harm. As he turned the corner he froze. An old man, young man, and a boy stood on the informal stone stage in front of a huge audience that numbered in the thousands, with more pouring into the square all the time. The young boy's voice had stopped Jacob cold, not the spectacle. The words tugged at the very strings of his heart.

"You must change." The boy spoke loud and authoritatively, yet he delivered the words almost casually, no, he delivered them compassionately, "Change your heart and change your ways. Judgment for the wrongs of this world is standing at the door; your injustice, your turning a blind eye to the poor and the needy. We have come here to help you, to heal you, to show you the way home." Silently a small team joined them on the stage, forming a semi-circle behind them.

With more than a little difficulty Jacob glanced away and was no longer mesmerized. He walked on to the highway, where he thumbed a ride that took him nearly to the farm's gate. One of his many talents was to look like a person to whom you would want to give a ride. It was the same aura of trust that had granted him access to the farm, or was it more than an aura?

Chapter 21 - Back on the Farm

And the One who is seated on the throne said,
"Behold, I am making all things new!"
Write this down for it is not only true, but it is
worthy of your trust.

Revelation 21:5

When Jacob got to the farm, he found Beth swinging in the front porch swing. She tried, unsuccessfully, to look like she had not been waiting for him by pretending to be reading a book. He walked up on the porch, dropped his duffle, and sat next to her on the swing.

She looked up from the book, "Oh, Jacob, you're back. How was the city?"

Jacob tried not to smile, "It was okay. I was surprised at how much I missed this place." He did not add, "and you," which she undoubtedly waited for. She wore one of her best long dresses, an off-white muslin with soft pink roses, and she smelled divine. She did not normally wear makeup, but was wearing a light touch of it today, just enough to enhance her natural beauty. His heart raced a bit, but he had superb self-control.

"Well," she jumped up, "it will soon be supper and I must go help mother," and she swished into the house.

Jacob took a deep breath. He had not realized he had been actually holding it. *"Wow,"* he said to himself, *"she is really something."*

Dinner was wonderful. The amazing dinner surprisingly avoided any fish, meat, or poultry. They did eat eggs and dairy, and combined everything else into rich and healthy dishes.

"Hmmm, that was a dichotomy wasn't it? Rich and healthy at the same time," he thought and, yet, it was exactly that.

After supper they gathered in the living room and Juan Carlos told another story. Jacob found himself as mesmerized as he had been at the city square. The story began with Jesus, sitting, teaching in their temple. The religious leaders, who did not like Him at all, attempted to catch Him doing something wrong. They had brought to him a woman caught in the very act of adultery. How could they do that, catch her in the very act, unless one of them was her compliant partner? According to their Law she should be stoned to death, but they asked Him for His decision. They were trying to trick Him. He knelt down and wrote something in the sand. As they continued to press him for an answer, he stood up.

Jacob found himself hanging on every word.

Jesus said, "Whichever one of you is without sin, you may be the first to throw a stone at her," and he knelt down again and continued writing in the sand.

The eldest most respected of them stepped forward, stone in hand. When he finally realized what Jesus had said and saw what he had written both times in the sand, he dropped his stone onto the ground. One by one, all of them did likewise and walked away. Even those He had been teaching walked away, ashamed of themselves and what they had been planning. He remained alone with the woman, her head bowed. She wept silently.

He stepped up to her, reached out, lifted her chin, and said, "Woman…" Why did He call her woman? He could have called her adulteress or worse. Why woman? He was re-dignifying her. He continued, "Where are your accusers? Does no one condemn you?"

She looked around, saw they stood alone, "No one, Lord." Then she dropped her head again. She realized that He still stood there and He could condemn her.

He reached out, lifting her head again, looked deeply into her soul. "Neither do I condemn you. Go and sin no more."

It felt like a light burst forth in her heart. She had been looking for love in all the wrong places. Now, as she looked into His eyes, she realized she had found the love she longed for, love powerful enough that she need not go back to her life of sin. Jesus smiled, lovingly touching her cheek as she smiled gratefully in return. She turned, and began to walk away. Before she left the temple courtyard, she turned back one time to look at Him. He stood there, still smiling. He nodded, and she left.

Jacob found tears silently flowing down his cheeks. He never, ever cried. He could not remember the last time he had cried. About to feel ashamed, he noticed tears in everyone's eyes, including Juan Carlos'. *"Who is this Jesus?"* he thought to himself again.

Juan Carlos walked back into the dining room and brought the armed chair, the one that always sat empty at the end of the table. He brought it back into the living room with him. He set it down at the end of the semi-circle of chairs and couches where they sat in the living room, in the place where he had been standing as he spoke.

He sat on the floor in front of his wife seat and said, "Sometimes it helps to picture Jesus sitting here," he pointed to the empty chair, "as we talk to Him."

Jacob's astonishment grew as one by one they all talked to Jesus as though he sat right there in that chair. Each of them, in their own way, thanked Him for not condemning them for the wrong that they had done. They thanked Him for dying to remove their wrong, their sin, and for living to bring them back into relationship with God.

When they finished, Jacob found himself asking, "Can He do that for me?"

Beth sounded a bit shocked, but answered, "Yes, just ask Him to do it."

"How, how do I do that?" he stammered.

"Just talk to Him like He is here," she answered, "because He is."

It seemed a little ridiculous to talk to an empty chair, but when he started talking he found that he suddenly entered into something unbelievably profound. Someone was there as he said, "Jesus, please take away my wrong." He stopped, as he felt like huge weight lifted from his shoulders, "And bring me back into a relationship with God." Something new burst forth in his heart just like it had in the heart of the adulterous woman. Now he cried tears of pure joy, laughing at the same time, the entire family touching him and hugging him.

PART 7 -
CITY EXPLOITS

Chapter 22 - Signs and Wonders in the City

In the midst of the final evil and perverse generation a remnant will emerge from out of nowhere and bring heaven down to earth. They will perform signs and wonders that the Dragon cannot duplicate. Those who have eyes to see and ears to hear will respond to this, the final call to come home.

From the "Chronicles of the Apocalypse"

Everyone assembled before the Tree all sitting or, at least, in some form of repose. Their numbers had grown, as many had been added these last few weeks from previous exploits, and all were now fully experienced in the operation of their giftedness and ready for the final series of strategic exploits. They only needed to know how and where to deploy.

Chayeem spoke and His words that reverberated in every heart, "Today begins the final call to come home. This week will be the people's last chance to change their hearts, change their ways, and join us. Alathos has shown many of you the ten portals that lead to various parts of the city. We will launch simultaneous teams to each of those areas to exercise your gifts and call as many as are willing to come home. The teams will be deployed each day in three cycles of four-hour shifts each. The first shift will be between breakfast and lunch, the next between lunch and dinner, and the final one for the day will be after dinner. Although we are as prepared as we can be, some of you will not return. Some of you will be captured, some of you will be wounded, some of you will be killed, but you know that they can only wound and destroy your body. They cannot destroy you. You belong to Me!"

The throng raised its voice in joyful assent, ready to lay down their lives to provide the opportunity for as many as possible to come home.

Chayeem continued, "So, here is how we will select the first team. Think of a color. Picture it in your mind."

Many of them looked at one another questioningly, but then thought of a color anyway.

"Those who were thinking of the color blue, stand up," said the Tree.

Caleb raised his paw, "Light blue or dark blue?"

"Either one," chuckled the Tree.

"What about turquoise or aqua," ventured Caleb.

"Caleb!" There was a slight edge to Chayeem's voice.

"Yes, Sir!" and Caleb stood up.

"You are the Blue Team," sang Chayeem. "You will follow Aaron to the city center's portal where you will assist my two witnesses. Remember, I am with you and you have some of my angels traveling with you too." He paused for a moment while the Blue Team dispersed. Meezimore began a worship song. Piper joined in and harmonized. Soon the rest of the congregation was lost in worship.

As the song ended Chayeem sang, "Those who were thinking of red, stand up." An entire flock of assorted birds took flight.

Adam the Cog raised his paw, "Maroon?"

"How are your wings, Adam?" Adam lowered his paw. The Tree sounded more amused than exasperated, "You will all follow Azinath to the next portal. Those that were thinking pink stand up." Interestingly females, both human and animal comprised the entire team. "Todah will lead you and, Teedhar, would you please join them."

"Yes, my Lord," responded Teedhar. He probably would have joined them anyway as he rarely allowed himself to be separated from Todah.

"Green? You will follow Meshar. Yellow, Piper; Violet, Eleazar; and Black, go with Justice. Your targeted return is lunchtime. I will expect most of you back by then. You have My blessing on your adventure. May many return with you! The rest of you are dismissed to your morning duties."

They all departed, either following their leader to their respective portal or to their duties. All except Mishal. He walked up to Chayeem, sat down, and leaned his back against the Tree.

"I am sure you noticed that someone from your team accompanied each of the exploit teams," began the Tree.

"Yes, Sir," Mishal responded.

"I am very grateful for how well you have taught each of them to just be comfortable having conversations with Me," Chayeem continued.

"You're welcome, Sir," smiled Mishal.

"You remember in the ancient writings that Abraham was called 'the friend of God' and at one point Jesus, the Liberator, called his disciples His friends?" If words could hug, the tone of these words did. "I appreciate the honor associated with you calling me "Sir", and in public that is still appropriate, but when it's just you and I, you can drop the "Sir", because I call you my friend."

Large tears formed in Mishal's eyes. Nothing Chayeem could have said would have touched him deeper. "Thank you," he replied, dropping the "Sir" and smiling between his tears of utter joy.

"What would you like to talk about, my friend?" inquired the Tree smilingly.

Mishal could hardly speak, but he managed. "After this week, when the number of the redeemed is complete, it will become really difficult out there in the world, won't it?"

"Yes." Chayeem's voice held a great deal of sadness. "I will be forced to pour out my judgment. Destroying so many and so much is one of the hardest things I have ever done, but I will make a new heaven and a new earth. I hope that makes up for it." Mishal turned, put his arm around the Tree's trunk, and together they wept.

Chapter 23 - Releasing the Captives

Signs and wonders preceded them as they proclaimed liberty to the captives, release to those imprisoned.

From the "Book of the Last Call"

A aron, Anna, Zek, Jordan and the rest of the team emerged from the portal in a darkened alley one short block from the city center square. Zek went immediately invisible leaving Mocherah as the only visible angel, albeit in his human form. They could hear the commotion clearly in the next block as they quickly assembled and prepared to move. Jordan carried a large backpack of food and most of the others carried smaller packs of food or clothing. The fifteen of them walked right out into the middle of the street and proceeded to march unhindered to the square. The crowd simply parted before them. They took up a location behind Abdul, Hash, and an old man who stood on a stone stage in the middle of the square. They spread out in a semi-circle and turned outward to face the crowd.

The old man saw them coming and said to the other two, "We have company. The Tree sends us aid."

Smiles widened on Abdul and Hash's faces as they continued to call in chorus, "You have little time left to repent, change your hearts, change your ways, and be reconciled to God. The time is short, destruction is at hand, judgement is at the door."

The crowd moved closer to the fifteen, curious to see what they had brought with them. When they saw the food, chaos nearly broke out, but the peacemaker Selah stepped forward, lifted her hand, and the discord miraculously stopped. She said in a perfectly calm voice, "Please, stay right where you are and we will come to you. There is plenty for all."

Jordan looked questioningly at Aaron, as nearly five thousand people filled the square. Aaron smiled, "Well, we do have more than five loaves and two fish," and he blessed the food. Those with food packs swung them from their backs to their fronts as they walked into the crowd distributing food as they went. The tumult they had heard from a block away quickly quieted as people received the food.

Jordan came upon an obviously crippled man. He turned to the man's two friends who stood beside him and said, "Take your friend to that man." He pointed to Aaron and handed them each some leaf-wrapped food. Watching them come towards him, Aaron looked at them intently, cocked his head to the side, smiled, nodded, and when they came close enough he reached out and healed the man.

All three of them dropped to their knees and asked. "What else must we do?" they pleaded. Aaron shared with them what the Liberator had done for them and still wanted to do for them, and they believed in Him. He counseled, "Go home and bring back your family. We should be here again tomorrow." They left rejoicing.

The fifteen had returned and most of the people sat quietly and satiated in the square, a perfect audience. Hash began, "You have just eaten of a miracle. You saw how we only had a few bags of food, and yet all of you have eaten your fill. This is the God we serve. He is calling you to Himself, to leave this life and follow Him with us. It is as simple as that."

High on a rooftop, Kouta, Ben's general, crouched with his sharpshooter. "Up until now the two with the old man have seemed invincible, but what of these new people? Surely they are not shielded too. Shoot the tall man in the middle!" he commanded. The sniper took aim on Aaron and, as he slowly exhaled, pulled the trigger. Just before the report of the weapon, Mocherah stepped in front of Aaron, raising his arm. A light flashed, the crowd screamed, and panic ensued. Everyone tried to escape at the same time. Selah raised her hand again, but this time to no avail. The frightened crowd stampeded out of the square injuring many until Hash, Abdul, the old man, and the fifteen gifted stood alone. Mocherah looked down. The projectile lay at his feet, crushed as if it had encountered a wall.

Aaron reached out and placed a hand on Mocherah's shoulder, "Thank you, my friend. I assume that was meant for me?"

"So it would seem," replied Mocherah, "and you're welcome." The fifteen turned to face the three.

"Well, we have some food left for you," said Jordan, "if you would like to eat of the miracle too. We are supposed to return to the Sanctuary by lunchtime. There will be another team after lunch and one after dinner too."

The old man spoke, "We are very grateful for your assistance and that of the Great Chayeem. Our road here has been difficult and without much response as of lately, but that seems to be changing. We're glad you're here and thank you for the food. I am also glad that you seem to be protected like us." They all nodded. They introduced one another, shook hands and embraced. Then the fifteen left them and returned to the alley to travel back through the portal to the Sanctuary.

Chapter 24 - Recovery of the Ability to See

And they will finally see what they have longed to see. The sight which they lost will be recovered, the darkness will be swallowed up in a great light.

From the "Book of the Last Call"

Eleazar and the Violet Team had walked through a different portal into the city's slums. The people's rampant poverty was displayed in a cardboard village that now obscured a former city park. Its tenants lived from day to day on the scraps they could scavenge from the garbage cans of the restaurants in the neighboring strip malls. There was never enough food to go around and many of its inhabitants went to bed hungry each night. What they did find was often spoiled. In conditions that bordered on starvation, disease accompanied their malnutrition like night follows day. Hopelessness and despair kept them constant company.

Into this darkened world stepped the Violet Team. Eleazar, Julius, Judy, and the rest of the team had brought as much food as they could carry and as soon as Eleazar blessed it, Chayeem again began to multiply it to feed the hungry. They walked from cardboard shack to cardboard shack passing out food, soon leaving behind them a multitude of folk who no longer hungered. The inhabitants realized that, for the first time they could remember, they felt full. They emerged from their huts to meet in the meadow that doubled as their meager village square. The team, all except Julius and Judy, formed a semi-circle around Eleazar who stood on an upturned milk box.

Julius stood off to the right astonishing the youth with his magic tricks. They had all sat down in front of him after he had done his first trick. He had walked up to a young boy and fanned out his deck of cards in his two hands, "Pick a card, any card. Now show it to your friends. Okay, put it back in the middle of the deck." He shuffled the deck on his knee a number of times. He then had the lad hold the deck while he proceeded to pull the card he had picked from behind the lad's left ear and showed it to the kids who applauded. He continued to amaze them while Eleazar spoke to their parents.

"We have come," Eleazar spoke strongly without having to shout, "from a place we call the Sanctuary. It is a place of peace, wonder, and beauty for God manifests Himself there. If you will leave your old life behind, you may come with us to live there."

"There is no god but Adonis our chancellor," spoke one of the men angrily.

"And how is that working out for you?" responded Eleazar. "There is no poverty in the Sanctuary. If you would you rather follow a god who has given you this," he pointed all around him, "then by all means stay here."

A young woman stepped forward, obviously blind. "I would come, but I cannot see the way." She held the hand of a slightly older woman.

Judy took Eleazar's hand. "I was once blind too, but He healed me."

The older woman stepped forward. "Were you once hospitalized for a drug overdose and a head injury?"

"Why, yes I was," Judy responded. "It was the combination of the two that had made me blind."

"My name is Christine," she held out her hand. "I was with the priest who prayed for you. You were delivered of the effects of the drugs, but unfortunately left with the blindness."

Judy let go of Eleazar's hand and grasped Christine's hand as tears filled her eyes. "God later healed my blindness too."

"Well," the young blind woman interrupted, "no one has healed me of mine."

Judy let go of Christine's hand, looked to Eleazar and, when he nodded, spoke directly to the young woman. "May I touch your head?"

"Yes." the young woman said as she herself nodded.

Judy took the young woman's head in her hands, looked up as she declared, "Eyes, be opened in the name of Chayeem, the Great Tree," then let go of the woman's head.

The woman looked startled, blinked twice, then turned to the woman beside her, "Christine, I can see. I can see!" She began to weep, fell to her knees, and buried her head in Christine's legs as she continued to declare that she could see.

Suddenly they could hear a commotion begin at the outskirts of their cardboard village. The militia had arrived and started making their way towards the meadow. Eleazar took one look at them and said, "Those who would leave this life behind, follow us quickly." He jumped off the box, took Judy's hand, and the team headed off in the direction away from the soldiers. About twenty of the villagers, including the young formerly blind woman, some of the children, and Christine followed them. Two of the men from the team stayed behind to act as their rear guard. When the soldiers realized the people were fleeing, they shouted for them to stop, but the people did not comply. The leader ordered his men to fire on them. As the soldiers shouldered their weapons, the team's rear guard suddenly became two angels. Each stood at least ten feet tall with drawn swords that had been unseen when they appeared as men. As the soldiers fired, the angels' swords burst into flame, consuming the incoming bullets. The soldiers had lowered their weapons from their shoulders to see the carnage, but they saw none. They shouldered their weapons again. Suddenly, they all looked confused. Their leader ordered them to fire again, but the soldiers looked at one another like they could no longer see the fleeing people. The angels quickly retreated backwards, caught up to the rest as they left the village, and all walked back through the portal.

The Violet Team, the twenty villagers and their children, entered the Sanctuary. Alathos the centaur met them there. The villagers seemed unsure how to react, but then he smiled and all was well. He welcomed them and they all stood a moment in awe at the beauty of the place. Alathos and the Violet team then led them to the Tree.

On their way, Eleazar had a question of Alathos, "What of the villagers' Quicksilver bioelectronic chips? Won't their chips tell the Triparteum that the Sanctuary still exists and even lead them here?"

Eleazar had a good point, but Alathos' response quieted his fears. "One of the beneficial side effects of traveling through the portals is that the disruption to the space continuum also disrupts the function of the chips. They are essentially rendered inactive as though the individual has ceased to exist."

The villagers now stood in the presence of the Tree, and their awe increased as Chayeem spoke to them, "Welcome to my Sanctuary." They all instinctively knelt. Even the children knelt as the Tree continued, "I am Chayeem. I have prepared this place for you. Eleazar will take you to your homes and give you some further instructions on how we live here. Thank you for coming to meet me. I know you will find this place to be beyond your wildest dreams."

As it seemed their impromptu audience had ended, they all got up and milled around until Eleazar directed them to follow him for a bit longer. He took them to the cooking and dining facilities that faced their cottages and had them sit down. Eleazar then proceed to share with them a few things about the Sanctuary and how it was run before he released them to their individual dwellings until supper. After supper they would learn how they would be able to contribute to this new society the following day.

PART 8 - CONFRONTATION

Chapter 25 - Another Meteor

And falling from the skies, another Nephilim invades the confines of Earth…

From the "Book of the Apocalypse"

The Astro-Aeronautics division notified Dr. Gideon Anakim that another meteor had crashed, this time in northern Sweden, and that a helicopter stood by to take him there. According to the reports, the initial scanning showed a composite similar to the one in which he had discovered the Gideonite. His pulse quickened as he quickly packed the instruments he would need, grabbed one of his assistants, and met the vehicle out on the lawn in front of his laboratory complex, its rotors still turning. He wanted to contact Science Director Adrian Quick, but it would have been premature without more evidence. An uneventful trip led to the site of a still smoldering crater. The area had been cordoned off by the Army and a place hastily cleared to act as their helipad. He exited the copter as soon as it touched down and his aide grabbed the instruments and quickly followed. For safety, they both donned hazmat suits and approached the meteor.

They estimated that about half of it had imbedded itself underground as they knelt on the warm earth around it taking their readings.

"Wow, some of the readings are off the chart!" thought Gideon excitedly. There was definitely something highly unusual about this meteor too.

The Army had responded to this event with amazing speed. They had a backhoe-like piece of equipment there with pincers instead of a bucket and a crate ready that appeared to be the right size to contain the meteor. Satisfied with their initial measurements and readings, Gideon supervised their picking it up and carefully depositing it in the crate. They quickly secured the lid, attached the cabling and, before you knew it, they headed back to the lab with their new discovery suspended below the copter. All of this they accomplished with as much secrecy as possible. Considering the size of the operation, the military had been involved to help keep it all under wraps.

When they arrived back at Gideon's laboratory complex, a lone flatbed awaited them in the now empty parking lot with another small contingency of Army personnel surrounding it. They positioned the crate on the flatbed. The soldiers detached the cables and then the copter landed in the empty parking lot beside it. Gideon and his aide quickly left the copter, climbed into the truck, and rode with the driver back into a hanger attached to the rear of the lab.

While his assistant stowed their equipment, another technician operated the overhead crane that removed the crate from the flatbed, opened it, and deposited it on a dolly. When the empty flatbed left the facility, Dr. Gideon took a few moments to key in the dolly's destination on his handheld device. He pressed "send," and off it went. The dolly followed an electronic pathway installed in the floor of the lab. They took a short cut through the lab, discarded their hazmat suits, and donned clothing for the "clean room" in which the meteor now rested. By the time they arrived, more technicians had operated the cranes in that room to remove the meteor and place it on what looked like a large operating table.

Gideon watched a three dimensional display created by a device that was a hybrid of x-ray, gamma-ray, and a CAT scan. He used a laser scalpel to grant him access to the meteor's liquid core. He removed a small portion of it and placed it in a test tube that he transferred to a multi-function scanning device for further evaluation. The results rapidly displayed on a screen in front of him.

"Yes! It is confirmed," he said as he turned to his assistant. "Please contact Director Quick for me." He continued reading, evaluating, and absorbing the impact of the results. Almost immediately his handheld device vibrated on his belt.

He touched his earpiece. "Dr. Anakim here."

It was Director Quick. "Gideon, I hear you have some good news for me."

"Yes, Adrian, we have just entered a new element into the Periodic Table. It was taken from another meteor. I am calling it 'Adonamite' in honor of the chancellor. If you would like to let him know of its discovery?"

"Certainly, gather all the information that you can and forward it to me on my secure channel. I will present this wonderful discovery to him in our morning briefing. Congratulations, my friend." And the Director rang off.

Chapter 26 - The Enemy's New Weapon

And the Dragon will discover an ancient source of immense power, whose properties will baffle all but a few. Yet one will arise to harness the element into a most strategic weapon of singular penetration using sorceries as old as time itself…

From the "Book of the Apocalypse"

They balanced on the edge of a precipitous moment the evening before "All Saints Day" on the Christian calendar. Much of the rest of the world still called it Halloween, or in Gaelic "Samhain" or "Sauln" when the the fairies Aos Si demanded appeasement. This year it coincided with the lunar eclipse of a blue moon, the second full moon of the month, and an unusual alignment of most of the planets. An evening like this had not occurred for thousands of years. Doctor Anakim joined Director Quick at the home of chancellor Adonis, his son the humanoid, Ben, and his prophet/medium, Baalel, for dinner. They had eaten a lavish meal, although the meat had seemed more raw than rare. After copious amounts of wine, most of them appeared a little inebriated. Adonis had punctuated the evening with a great deal of praise for all of their recent accomplishments.

"But," he proclaimed, "those were nothing compared to what the future holds." He predicted, "Tonight, we stand on a threshold of a greatness, the likes of which the world has never seen!" Ben walked around the table refilling their wine glasses. "I want you to all accompany me to my personal sanctuary. Bring your wine glasses." He stood up and the rest of them joined him.

He led them down into his underground bunker until they came to a luxuriously ornate door covered in occult signs and symbols. They stopped in front of it, and the doctor and director suddenly felt very cold. They shivered in unison, unsure whether to attribute it to the cold or the palatable fear that also gripped them. Baalel had grabbed his staff as they left the dining room and said something unintelligible before touching the door inscribed with occult symbols that stood before them. The door simply disappeared and they walked down into an even more penetrating cold and a near darkness. The room they entered contained a black stone altar table.

"Place your wine glasses on the altar," he said commandingly. Baalel stepped around the altar to its other side. He set down his glass, drew a dagger, and sliced his palm. He then squeezed a few drops of his blood into his wine and stirred it with the bloodied blade. He proceeded to pour some of his wine into each of the other glasses. "Now," Adonis further commanded them all, "drink the contents of your glass completely!"

The doctor and the director looked briefly at each other and then drank all of the contents of their individual glasses, as did everyone else. Off to the left, just outside of their peripheral vision, a flash of light illuminated the hallway to another room.

Ben questioned, "Father, has that room always been there?"

"Yes, my son," he replied, "but inaccessible until now. Come!" He led the way.

They walked into a large antechamber. In the center of the room stood another black stone altar table and an angel of indescribable light and beauty. They found it difficult to remain standing, so they all fell to their knees.

The being spoke and it seemed all the music of the world echoed in his words, although in a somewhat minor key. "You may remain kneeling if you would like, but I believe you will be more comfortable if you regain your feet."

With difficultly they all stood and for the first time noticed that there were objects on the table. It looked like rounds of ammunition, a lot of ammunition. The being reached over and grasped a container. Gideon recognized it as the container of Adonomite that the chancellor had asked him to bring to the dinner. He had wondered what had happened to it.

The being continued, "Thank you, doctor," his piercing gaze nearly unhinged the doctor, "for discovering this." His laughter contained quite another kind of glee, almost maniacal. "It had been hidden beyond even my ability to see."

He lifted the container, unscrewed its top, and proceeded to pour most of its contents over the ammunition. The strangest thing happened. It looked like the bullets soaked up the Adonomite completely with nothing left over. Then the angel drew his sword, one of the original singing swords gifted to the archangels. When he drew it, the song it produced had them all immediately on the floor in convulsions, except Ben whose non-human traits somehow afforded him protection. The angel poured the last of the Adonomite over the sword without spilling a drop and then laid it across his palms. The music stopped and their convulsions with it. They weakly regained their feet once again. Ben remained standing almost regally.

The being stepped forward, "The last time we met, Ben, two of my angels gave you their swords, which you swallowed. This sword is mine and I lend it to you for the duration of this coming conflict. It will sing for no one but you and me. Use it well in my service."

This time Ben took a knee and extended his hands to receive the sword, which the angel handed him. He rose and sheathed it.

"Wait," thought the doctor, *"where did the sheath come from?"* Before the doctor could voice his astonishment, a portion of the wall behind the angel of light slid back and revealed two bound angels. He could not tell what bound them, but bound they were, with their hands immobilized behind them. They shifted back and forth from their human form, as men over six feet tall, to their angelic form, ten feet tall with wings and all, and then back to their human form again. Their constant shifting made it difficult to focus on them, tell if they writhed in pain or if they were intensely vainly trying to free themselves. Whatever the angels were feeling, it filled the room with something like fear, but subtly different. The angel of light stepped to the side of the altar, reached down and produced a rifle.

He loaded one of the rounds that had soaked up the Adonomite into it and handed it to Ben, "You know how we have been plagued for months by a few individuals in the city center square who have seemed invincible and were protected by angels? It is difficult to destroy angels, but the solution," he laughed at the pun concerning the Adonomite, "is at hand." He looked at Ben, who put the rifle to his shoulder and shot the first angel. The angel disintegrated into dust. "And my newly anointed sword?" He asked as he again nodded to Ben. Ben laid the rifle on the altar and drew the sword. It made absolutely no sound now at all. Suddenly, it seemed to sing with the absence of sound. Ben stepped forward and skewered the remaining angel and it too dematerialized.

The Luminescent One smiled, "Now, off to war with you!" and he disappeared from view.

Chapter 27 - The Return of the Blue Team

And the Dragon will wage war against My two witnesses, but shall not prevail for a time. Rather, they will appear invincible to all of his attacks until the time is complete.

From the "Book of the Last Call"

The Blue Team's turn came again to go reach out to those in the city who still had not heard the call to turn from their waywardness, change their hearts, change their ways, and flee the wrath to come by following the team to God's Sanctuary. Led by Aaron and joined by Anna, Zek, Jordan, and Mocherah, the rest of the team simply walked through the portal like it was an every day occurrence stepping into their now familiar alley. Zek went invisible again, leaving Mocherah in his human form. They joined Hash, Abdul, and the old man in the square as they declared the good news that the Liberator had come to change everything, to make all things new.

Crowds of people quickly gathered in the square and formed into a number of convenient lines. While the limited supply of clothing depleted quickly in the food and clothing line, the dispensing of food again multiplied. Hopefully the people would not take this almost daily amazing occurrence for granted. The sick, the blind, the deaf, and the lame formed a somewhat less formal line that was still orderly. The team walked among them, touching them, comforting them, joining them on the ground, and healing them. Spectators beheld wonderful light in the spiritual darkness of the city, as though a piece of heaven had showed up on earth for a brief time to bring hope and wholeness.

Then, as usual, the Triparteum militia arrived. They formed ranks at the end of the square, a line of them kneeling with rifles to their shoulders, and a second line standing behind them, also with their rifles to their shoulders. Not usual was the ten-foot tall form of Ben Ha-Chiya-Ra standing behind them. The army had failed so often in their near-daily confrontations that neither the crowds, the Blue Team, nor the old man and the two witnesses took any notice of them. Only Mocherah stepped through the crowd to stand alone and face them. When the army fired on them, Mocherah had always proven able to render their attack ineffective. Mocherah had faced Ben before and always proved equal to the task, but something differed today. When Ben drew his sword everything changed. It seemed as though time stopped, all the air sucked out of the square, and a horrible stillness filled the vacuum left behind. Mocherah drew his own sword and it shimmered in the stillness, but the dark sword of the false angel broadcast some kind of elemental disharmony. Ben and Mocherah both stepped forward to engage each other. Mocherah attempted, unsuccessfully, to block and parry the false angel's powerful thrust. Mocherah's sword shattered into a thousand fragments, and Ben's sword pierced him clean through. Mocherah eyes widened and suddenly, he imploded and vanished. All eyes turned to where only a moment before he had stood valiantly defending them, and a cry of anguish filled the air. The false angel raised his sword and shouted "fire" as he brought it back down, pointing at the two witnesses. The sound of the volley accompanied hundreds in the crowd falling slaughtered to the ground, including the two witnesses.

General panic ensued and everyone began running in all directions. Only a few remained standing including Anna and Aaron. Aaron ran to where the two witnesses, Hash and Abdul, lay mortally wounded. The old man had been shot too, but superficially. The shock of the two lads fallen at his feet had immobilized him. Aaron grabbed him, lifted him, and sprinted across the square carrying him towards the portal. The soldiers attempted to cut them off. The old man seemed to shake off his stupor, escaping Aaron's grip. They heard the single report of another weapon, a melodious clang as it was deflected, and there stood Zemir in all of his angelic glory, the singing sword Hashamayeem swinging in circles all around him. He marched into the army's ranks, cutting a path as he backed towards the portal Aaron mystified at Zemir's appearance, stepped with him and together they turned as they reached the portal. The false angel Ben had taken flight towards them. Aaron walked through the portal while Zemir turned once more and faced the false angel Ben, who had landed soundlessly to stand in front of him. A fierce battle ensued. It was astonishing to behold. Thrusts, cuts, parries, counters, bashing and clashing as the dark met the light, the false encountering the true, with a final triumphant chord as Hashamayeem met the dark blade's soundless note, Zemir too backed through the portal. Ben tried to follow him into it, but the portal no longer existed or at least was not open to him.

He turned back to the decimated crowd and there alone stood Anna, surrounded by half a dozen burley-armed soldiers. "Take her, but do not harm her!" he commanded. "I will take care of her myself."

They roughly grabbed her. Ben strode off towards their compound and the soldiers dragged Anna after him. Once there, they took her to a block of cells downstairs and roughly threw her into one. "The Master will attend to you shortly," one said and they all joined in mocking laughter.

Anna crumpled onto a cot in the corner sobbing. *"What has happened?"* she thought as she cried, *"Until moments ago it had seemed we were invincible, and then our protection disappeared like a mist. Have we been abandoned?"*

Suddenly she found herself fully embraced as Zek materialized and comforted her. "No, we are not forgotten, but this is a war and some battles are lost. Take heart, little one, and recall all that He has done for us." In a blink he was gone again, but he had staunched the tears, and hope began to replace them.

She sat up, wiped her face, and softly said, "Thank you." Lapsing into unconsciousness and wonderful dreams of home, the Sanctuary, and all of her friends. She awoke a few days later as she heard footsteps coming down the stairs. Her faith and courage fully restored, she rose ready to face whoever appeared.

Chapter 28 -
Upping the Stakes

And they were victorious over their enemies because the Liberator's death had already cleansed them, because they testified to His love and power, and because they were prepared to die even as He had died.

From the Revelation 12:11

The Sergeant brought Anna before Lieutenant Torbid. She had only been unconscious in that prison cell for a few days, to grotesque effects. She could barely stand and she smelled of something terrible. The Sergeant stepped back from her, wiped his hand on his pant leg in disgust, and drew his pistol. The Lieutenant standing in front of her drew his pistol also. Anna smiled weakly.

The Lieutenant sneered, "You think this is funny? I have the power of life and death over your miserable self. I can snuff your life out with a single shot!"

Anna took a ragged breath, "No sir, you cannot," she whispered. "You may destroy this body, but I will live on. Over that you have no control."

The Lieutenant continued, "Recant your belief in this so called Liberator and I will spare your wretched life! How can you still trust in a man who has left you blind? Adonis would heal you of your blindness if you would simply worship him. Recant, you fool, recant and turn to the only one who can save you."

Anna slowly took another breath and stood taller, "You think that I am blind, but it is you who cannot see. Do you see this angel standing with me? No, you don't! I definitely will not recant!" Zek placed his arm around her shoulder and she drew strength from his touch.

"You fool!" He spat out the words now, "There is no one here to save you, no angel, no Liberator!" He pointed his pistol at her and pulled the trigger. Nothing happened, save an empty click. "Sergeant, kill the girl!"

Reluctantly, the Sergeant raised his weapon and pulled the trigger. Again, just a click. He looked at his gun. It seemed fine.

The Sergeant pointed his gun at Anna once again and pulled the trigger. Just before it discharged Anna bent over in a coughing spasm. Her time in the cold and dank cell seemed to have brought on some illness. When her cough subsided, she looked up at the Lieutenant. He was holding his hand to his chest, blood beginning to seep through his fingers.

"You shot ME...you idiot!" Torbid said to the Sergeant; then he crumpled to the floor.

Astonished, the Sergeant looked at his weapon, dropped it to the ground, and fled from the scene. *"At least they had time to plant the enhanced tracker in her clothing while she was unconscious in her cell,"* he thought as he ran.

"Well, Zek, the door is open. Do you suppose we should just leave?" Anna ventured. Zek smiled, picked her up, and carried her to the portal and home.

PART 9 - THE FINAL SOLUTION

Chapter 29 - The Sanctuary Lives

How can they respond if they cannot see the attack coming? When you combine secrecy, stealth, and the cover of darkness, you have created a virtually unbeatable combination.

From the "Strategies of War"

A donis, Ben, and Baalel met once again in the chancellor's unholy subterranean meditation center that lay beyond the occult doorway. They had gone down the stairs and now stood before the black altar.

Ben had reported that although the blind girl had escaped, she had carried with her a newly-developed tracker, and it had indicated that the enemy still used the location of the original sanctuary as its headquarters. He had deployed troops to reopen the collapsed entrance and they should soon be able to enter.

"Thank you, my son," Adonis had spoken, so pleased that he had actually placed a hand on Ben's neck and gently caressed it. Ben could never remember his father ever doing that before. Surely, when he was young, maybe. Years before the auto accident he must have done it. It felt so familiar, so right.

They each had sliced their own palm this time and squeezed some of their blood to mingle in the bowl on the altar. Baalel continued with his unintelligible incantations, but seemingly to no avail. No answering light flashed, no angelic being appeared. Perhaps their confidence had been shaken, their belief in the unalterable victory of their cause. While they had killed the two witnesses and a number of angels, the witnesses had come back to life three days later. Ben, fighting with the angel of light's own soundlessly singing sword, had been fought to a standstill by another mere angel. Baleel shouted louder, cut himself deeper and still nothing. Finally, he collapsed writhing on the floor. Adonis and Ben looked at one another questioningly. Ben drew the sword belonging to the luminescent angel of light and laid it on the altar as well. With a sudden muffled concussion, the dark angel of light appeared before them although not quite visible. It seemed he could not, for the moment, fully materialize on this plane, as if something was preventing him. With another muffled "Whump" he finally stood before them. Baalel had stopped moving at the angel's feet. The angel of light reached down, grabbed Baalel by the throat with one hand and clumsily deposited him on the altar, knocking off both the bowl and the sword. He picked up the sword, cut off the prophet's hand, and proceeded to eat it raw, dropping the sword back on the floor.

All the indescribable beauty that stood before them on other occasions suddenly tarnished. Reality and truth wavered like a desert mirage. They shook their heads almost in unison and rubbed their eyes in an attempt to dispel whatever they saw, trying to return to normal.

"What do you want!" the being hissed, as an intense pain filled the room.

"My Lord," Adonis whimpered, "We have discovered the enemy's camp. That place that we thought we had once destroyed has been resurrected into their current headquarters."

"Argh…" the being squirmed as if struck with a physical blow "You would use that word in my presence? *Resurrected?*" And he spat a finger on the ground! "Next you will use the name of that infernal imposter himself!" He spat another finger on the ground. "The Son of God," he sneered, "You must gain entrance to that place, enter it, and destroy it."

"That is why we summoned you, my lord," ventured Ben, "we are, even now, reopening the entrance to it. We need to know what we should do next?"

"How should I know that, you fool!" the dark angel cried out in frustration. "I cannot see it. I do not even know where it is. This entire planet lies within my power, soon the entire universe, but that is the one place outside of my dominion and beyond my vision." Suddenly it was like a sun dawned in his mind. "That is it! Gain me entrance into that place and it all will become mine,"

In a blink he was gone and for the moment it seemed like he had taken all the air with him.

"Well," Adonis struggled to breathe and to say, "I'm not sure how productive all that was."

"I don't understand," questioned Ben, "has the Luminescent One been weakened somehow?"

Adonis replied, "It felt as though we are laboring under some kind of interference, but know this, our victory is assured. We will do as he has commanded. We will enter their camp and provide the way for him to follow."

He reached down, picked up the bowl, placing the two dismembered fingers in it. Ben retrieved the fallen sword.

"Hmmm," Ben thought to himself gratefully, *"he didn't take back the sword, so I guess it is mine for a little longer."* He could think of nothing he liked in his hand more. He touched the bowl with the tip of the blade and its contents burst into flame. Baalel still lay unconscious on the altar. They thrust the stump of his arm into the bowl to cauterize it.

"Aaagh...." that brought him back to life. He cradled the stump in his other hand as he whimpered, "My hand, my hand, what happened to my hand?"

"You gave it to the Luminescent One. He accepted it as a sacrifice." He neglected to tell him that the dark one had cut it off himself and then proceeded to eat it raw.

"And...he was pleased? He...accepted my sacrifice?" A small wicked smile crept across Baalel's face, as though the loss of his hand might be worth it.

"Yes, I believe that he was," Adonis lied. The dark one had not been pleased about anything, except the small chance that they might be able to enter and destroy the enemy's lair. "We need a plan!"

Chapter 30 - Strategies and Tactics

The only tactic that trumps betrayal is an adequate distraction accompanied by deception. Of course, there is always the use of brute force.

From the "Strategies of War"

Kouta, and another Lieutenant, Molek, entered the council chambers and each took a knee in front Ben and Adonis.

"We have some good news, and we have some bad news," began Kouta. Adonis nodded for them to continue as Kouta stood, "First the bad news. The two bastard children of the Virgin that we slew in the city square lay dead for three days, which were marked by one of the greatest celebrations in recent times. Well, this morning, with the rising of the sun, a strong wind blew through the square and they stood up. It seemed the wind made them alive again. The wind then circled around them, lifted them from the ground, and took them off into the clouds. Our drones were unable to follow them because of the turbulence of the wind."

"We knew that already!" snapped Ben.

"There has been no sign of them. They did not return to preach today in the city center," Kouta continued.

"And that's the good news?" Ben sneered.

"No!" responded Kouta, "there is better news than that."

"Ah," interjected Adonis, "then join us at the table."

They sat in a council of war around a three dimensional, natural color, topographical representation of the enemy's lair. Baalel muttered his normal unintelligible incantations off in the corner and burned some foul-smelling incense, all the while stroking his stump.

"Our excavation teams assured me that we will be ready to enter the cavern tomorrow," Kouta had retaken the floor, "but I was wondering if it would be a better strategy to wait until darkness sets in before we enter?"

Ben stood and nearly shouted in exasperation, "It's a cavern. While they must have some kind of internal lighting, torches, fires, or something, I doubt they have the technology for artificial lighting. Outside darkness is probably inconsequential."

"Yes sir," continued Kouta, "On the other hand, we have used only manual, slave labor to remove the rocks and debris and this has been done relatively quietly, with the utmost caution, so we should still have the element of surprise."

Ben smiled, "That was good thinking, Kouta. I'm proud of you for thinking of that." Kouta also smiled, for being appreciated, especially in front of the chancellor. "Do we have any idea where their center of operations is, once we are inside?

"The tracker that the blind girl is carrying should give us her location once we are inside too," said Kouta, "and hopefully lead us there without her knowing it."

Adonis sneeringly and cruelly spoke again, "How appropriate that she should betray them into our hand without ever knowing that she is doing so."

"How large of an attack force should I assemble?" asked Ben. "Do we want to hit them with everything we've got?"

"No," Adonis mused, "I think it would be more effective and efficient if you used a small, quick attack team of our most adept and elite forces. How many of the new winged vests do we have?"

Ben replied, "I think, besides the one designed to fit me, there are six other normal-sized vests, and even those can be reconfigured easily."

"Ah," sighed Adonis smiling, "just right. The enemy's perfect number, seven. So, besides you, me, Kouta, and Molek, we only need three others of our most elite supermen. Do we still have enough ammunition left that the dark lord blessed with Adonomite?"

"Yes, Father," added Ben, "we recovered most of the rounds we used in the attack that initially killed the two witnesses and we have prepared it for reuse. Although we have little idea of the size of the enemy's force, we should have more than enough to destroy at least their leadership and then as many as we can until we run out of the anointed ammunition. If we cut off the Virgin's head, the rest will either run or surrender anyway. They are not trained for war as we are. Then Ben added, "Father, I am somewhat surprised you are not taking Baalel with us."

"Baalel is no longer fit for service, He lost more than his hand to the dark lord. I think he also lost what was left of his sanity. He has definitely outgrown his usefulness," said Adonis shortly. "Let's finish our preparations and meet at the entrance site at 0600," and he adjourned their war council.

Chapter 31 - Battle Plans

The use of a small force aids your ability to achieve speed, secrecy, and surprise.

From the "Strategies of War"

Today they would finally do what they had trained for all these years. Known collectively as the Terrors, the trio wielded every size, shape, and kind of weapon. Their hand-to-hand combat skills set them still further apart. They could kill you with anything they had at hand, with just their hands, or with nothing at all. They all excelled in the use of psychic force, the harnessing of supernatural energy. If they could get close enough, they could and would eliminate a target with ruthless efficiency and without a second thought. While not nearly as imposing as the chancellor's son, Ben, both J1 and J2 stood over six feet tall. What their third partner lacked in size and strength, she made up for in her cat-like quickness. In fact, they had nicknamed her Cat and swore she had the nine lives to go with it. She had escaped numerous assignments as the lone survivor. Their training this week had culminated in the use of the winged vests. While still technically in the prototype stage, what they had learned to accomplish using them nearly bordered on the miraculous.

All seven of them met at the site of the entrance to the cavern at 0600 as planned. They strapped on their winged vests and proceeded into the now cleared opening. Once inside, the pathway appeared virtually unobstructed, although they proceeded carefully. They walked for about a mile, though their stealthy pace made it seem longer than that. J1, J2, and Cat led the way, followed by Ben and Adonis with Kouta and Molek as their rear guard. One moment they crept through the cave, the next, they stood in a forest, struggling to adjust their sight to the light of day. They had emerged ready and wary, but no one guarded the entrance. Apparently, the forest's inhabitants believed the cave's entrance was still blocked.

Kouta placed the ear buds in his ears and activated the tracking device. It clearly showed the girl's location about two clicks straight ahead of them.

"This shows us that she is about two clicks in front of us," Kouta whispered back over his shoulder as he turned to take two small drones out of Molek's backpack. "We'll stay here until our reconnaissance drone has scouted out the area and is in position," and he threw one of them into the sky. It left them quickly, silently, and then before entirely out of sight seemed to disappear. While they waited, they spread out, relieved themselves, and came back together to share some energy bars and some bottled water they had brought along with them. Almost before they knew it there was a "beep" and the second drone took off.

"Report!" commanded Kouta.

They had now gathered in a circle. The second drone shared with them a composite three-dimensional compilation from the video images that the first drone captured as it flew ahead of them. This it projected as a holographic image in the middle of them as the second drone hovered about six cubits above them. The image's clarity and composition astounded them all. In the center of the image a pillar of fire reached from the ground all the way up and into the lens where the drone's projection originated. Around the pillar a series of small cottages and other buildings spread out. In a large open field in front of the pillar nearly a thousand people appeared assembled, but on further examination the mass of people consisted of humans, animals, mythical beings (including centaurs), and what appeared to be angels. Around the pillar stood twelve individuals, not all human either. One individual looked like a genetic atrocity, part dog and part cat. Another was the blind girl who had escaped from them.

"Hmm," mused Adonis, "part of this will be easier than we thought. I don't see any offensive or defensive weapons other than the largest centaur has a bow and some arrows. The biggest question is, what do you suppose is the purpose of that huge and unnatural fire? Is it some sort of energy source, powering whatever lights up this underground forest?'"

Ben added, "And why are there twelve individuals surrounding it? It's almost as if they are somehow protecting it. Kouta could you zoom in on one of the individuals surrounding the pillar?"

Kouta touched his throat transmitter and had the drone comply.

"Wait!" exclaimed Cat, Isn't that Gomed? He used to be one of us." Kouta zoomed in closer and Gomed looked up directly into the camera. "I think he spotted us." She exclaimed.

"That's not possible," replied Kouta, "the drone is cloaked, it's invisible."

"Not to Gomed and his accursed proximity sense," hissed Cat. "He has something hidden in his right hand. Is it a weapon?»

"I can't tell, but we need to attack quickly before we fully lose the element of surprise," said Ben. "Cat, as our best marksman, position yourself here," and he pointed to a small hill in the projected display, "as we fly in and land before the fire. On my command shoot the 'atrocity'," and he pointed to the Cog. "Then we will see how they respond."

"Yes, sir," Cat replied.

"Then, let's lock and load, and be off," said Kouta.

They flew in the same tight formation as they had earlier traveled except with Cat trailing them and dropping down to the hill as they passed over it. She quickly set herself up as they continued flying. The assembly began to look up, with some excited exclamations and some pointing. The attack force landed between the congregation and the pillar of fire that the twelve still surrounded.

PART 10 - CAUSE AND EFFECT

Chapter 32 -
One Shot Victory

What was once opened will be closed, and what was once closed will be opened again.

From the "Whispers in the Dark"

Chayeem had called for a solemn assembly. The entire congregation had responded and stood before the Pillar of Fire where the Tree usually stood, but for some reason stood no longer. For that very reason they reluctantly came into the assembly grounds. The earlier word that had been spoken, "The Tree will be located outside of My Pillar because the people feel more comfortable talking to it than they do to Me in this pillar," had been fulfilled and now seemingly revoked.

He now addressed the people from the Fire and every heart rang full with His words, "The enemy is about to launch an attack on us, so I have moved the Tree back inside of My Pillar for its protection.

Caleb raised his paw, "Can't the Tree protect Himself?"

The Pillar chuckled, as Chayeem would have. He was very fond of that dog too. "Normally, yes, but today is special. I would ask the twelve to please assemble about my circumference and take up their stones."

The twelve responded and did as He asked, each in their own special way. The men, women, and angel picked up their stones in their right hands. Adam, the Cog, picked up his between his paws, and Dal, the hawk, had his, for the moment, in his beak. Meshar's proximity sense tingled. He looked up and spotted the enemy's cloaked surveillance drone.

"They're in the Sanctuary," he blurted out.

"Yes, they are coming, from the East," a great sadness engulfed His words, "but one is no longer with them."

The assembly looked up to see the six enemies flying in formation. Some pointed, others exclaimed. The six landed in the space between the people and the pillar.

Adonis announced to the people, "There is no need for bloodshed," he lied. With a slight chop downward of his hand, Adam virtually exploded at the impact of the bullet, followed almost immediately by the report from Cat's rifle. His stone clattered to the ground and the Pillar of Fire extinguished to reveal the Tree, the Ark, and the two angels that protect the Ark. The two angels fell backwards to the ground as two more cracks of the rifle sounded in near unison,

"Can we do nothing?" someone yelled. Meshar responded. He drew his sword and faced J1 and J2, who were flanked by Kouta and Molek. The four pulled revolvers and tried to shoot him, but their guns jammed. J1 and J2 dropped their guns and pulled knives. Another rifle crack resounded, but Meshar had already deflected the bullet meant for him with a simple defensive movement of his sword.

"Zek?" Anna pleaded for help.

With the stone of Peace now in his left hand and the sword of Peace in his right, Meshar attacked the two J's. With a flurry of sword and knives clashing Meshar disarmed them both and left them unconscious on the ground before them all. The ferocity and speed of Meshar's attack so astounded Kouta and Molek that they just stood there immobilized. He knocked them unconscious too and then re-sheathed his sword.

Ben looked at Adonis and spoke concerning Mesha, whom he had known as Gomed when he still served the Triparteum, "Gomed was always our best..." he left the sentence hanging. Things no longer proceeded according to their plans. Then everything changed again.

A loud, totally discordant note sounded. A shimmering and disorienting portal opened in front of the Tree, and out stepped the Luminescent One. He had been called simply "Hal" before the beginning of time, but soon he would be called god. He dangled Baalel from one hand like a rag doll. When he dropped Baalel at his feet, Baalel staggered, trying to stay erect by hanging on to the staff in his good hand.

Just then Alathos rode up with Zek on his back, and with Cat bound and draped behind Zek. In one fluid movement Zek dismounted and dropped Cat into the unconscious pile of J1, J2, Kouta, and Molek.

Hal had turned to face Alathos and Zek. He scowled, turned back towards the Tree and the Ark, and reached out his right hand towards Ben. Ben handed him back his singing sword. Hal, Adonis, and Ben advanced past the Tree with Baalel continuing to stagger behind them. Hal carelessly loped off a fruit-laden branch as they passed it by. Baalel tripped over the tree branch and collapsed. The unholy trio continued on towards the Ark of God with the two angels lying fallen beside it, intent on destroying the Ark. Alathos fired an arrow at Adonis' back, but Ben quickly turned to pluck it out of the air, in mid-flight. He crushed it in his hand like a soda straw.

Ben took a deep breath, but before he could speak, Zemir, Meshar, and Todah began singing a powerful, yet beautiful song of worship and all the eleven joined in. The worship immobilized the unholy trio for a moment. Retching, Ben vomited up his dark sword of power, causing him to lose the ability to destroy things with sound. Ben, still shaking his bewildered head, picked up the vomit-covered sword. Hal handed his darkened singing sword to Adonis and raised his arms, about to conduct the final chord of his entire unholy life's symphony.

Time seemed to slow to a near stop as Adonis and Ben raised their swords to strike the Ark and ten of the eleven gasped in chorus. But Anna had placed her stone in her blouse, had run forward, picked up two of Chayeem's fruit, and threw them at the back of Adonis' and Ben's heads. At that same moment, unnoticed and behind all of their backs, a small mound of dirt appeared next to Adam's remains, where the fallen Discernment stone lay. Diggory the gopher popped out, picked up the fallen stone and joined Anna as she regained her place in the circle and took her stone back out of her blouse. The Pillar re-ignited. Normal time restarted and the twelve placed their stones back in their receptacles and entered the pillar. The fruit that Anna thrown had hit Ben and Adonis squarely in the back of their heads. It had splattered and comically ran down their backs.

Covered in the awe of Chayeem they fell on their faces at the feet of the Ark. Hal found himself immobilized, as the two covering angels were restored to once again stand beside the Ark of God. Led by Zemir, Meshar, and Todah, the rest of the twelve slowly walked around Hal, Baalel, who had finally caught up with the others and fallen on his own face, Adonis, and Ben. With their worship, they began to weave a series of impenetrable chains about each one of unholy four. As they finished all four were on their faces, bound before the Ark. The twelve stepped back in awe at the results of their worship.

Epilogue

These are those who conquered kingdoms, brought about justice, obtained what they asked, stopped animal attacks, quenched the fire, escaped the edge of the sword, were made strong in their weakness, became mighty in war, and put the enemy to flight.

Hebrews 11:33-34

The voice of God reverberated from the Ark and the Tree simultaneously. "You, O Dragon, your beast, its image and his false prophet shall remain here bound for the next one thousand years!" And the earth opened to swallow the four of them into the Abyss along with Kouta, Molek, Cat, J1 and J2.

As the earth closed back up, the twelve knelt before the Ark and the Tree to joined in another verse of the worship song that they thought they had completed moments before. The Pillar of Fire extinguished once again without even the hint or smell of residual smoke and God continued to speak as the entire assembly listened, "I repeat to you the charge I gave long ago. Be fruitful. Multiply all that you are and all that you do. Fill the earth with my image and bring it back into compliance. You have learned much here in my Sanctuary. You have experienced much here. You have found new friendships and begun new relationships. Now extend all of this to cover this world. I have plowed the earth clean. Together we will cultivate, plant, and harvest anew, spreading awe and wonder across the face of the planet.

A joyful cheer resounded from the solemn assembly, beginning at the Tree and moving throughout them all. As this glorious shock wave extended the entire assembly fell to the ground as if asleep. The two angels Ayah and Anan laced the poles into their receptacles on the Ark, hoisted it to their shoulders, and stepped through a portal. Meanwhile, the Tree nearly doubled in size becoming the prominent feature of the assembly area. The sleeping people, angels, animals, and all awakened to find the underground Sanctuary no longer under ground but bathed in the purest sunlight any of them could recall.

Aaron stood, as did the rest of the twelve, and said, "We have our orders, a world to reclaim. Let's get to it."

Caleb raised a paw, "Can we have supper first?"

"A good idea," responded Aaron. "You can begin your planning as you eat your supper. And don't forget to include Chayeem in your planning."

As the assembly began to disperse to their cooking and dining facilities, José heard his name called from behind him and turned to find himself face to face with Christine Andrews, the young nurse from the hospital where he took Judy when she hit her head during a drug overdose. Judy's accident seemed like so long ago. Christine had stood there praying with him when Judy was delivered from the symptoms that should have accompanied her withdrawal from the drug overdose, but left her with blindness.

He smiled, "Christine, this is a wonderful surprise. How long have you been here?"

She smiled in return, "Not long. I tried to help at the hospital right up to the very end, the need was so great. I was serving in one of the slum areas when I encountered one of your final exploit teams. Judy was there and healed a young blind woman I had been helping. The militia attacked, but we made it through the portal in time. Our paths haven't crossed until now, but I have met a large talking pelican named Kate."

"Ah, Kate," if his smile could deepen, it did. "Isn't she a wonder?"

"Yes," for some reason she blushed, "we have become good friends. She talks a lot about you."

"She does? Only good, I hope," he reached out a hand. "Let's go have some supper. I think we have a lot of catching up to do."

She took his hand as her blush deepened even more.

About the Author

William (Bill) Siems

Bill has always been a storyteller. His wife says he still tends to share the truth creatively and with a flair for the dramatic. He grew up in south Seattle and has lived in Tacoma, Washington since 1972.

Initially working in hospitals (he completed half his RN education), Bill joined the Boeing Airplane Company in 1979. The last 15 years of his 32-year career he taught Employee and Leadership Development. Bill often developed and taught his own material and has written numerous short stories and dramas, culminating in his first published novel, "Amidst the Stones of Fire" in 2017.

Now retired, he spends his time teaching, mentoring, acting in community theater, and enjoying his family. Bill and his wife of more than fifty years, Nancy, live near their three children and six grandchildren.

If you can't find Bill in his home-office, he is probably across the street playing with the neighbor's dog.

Made in the USA
San Bernardino, CA
30 July 2018